To Sue
may this
bring you lots
of magic

INSIGHTS INTO THE NEXT REALM:
SHADOWS FROM THE DARKNESS

A NOVEL BY ERIKA RAVNSBORG

Contents

Prologue

There is no once upon a time in this story. It sounds trite to say once upon a time since this is a story that begins before once upon a time.

It all begins with a full gigantic tree that has several names. Bodhi, Kalpavriksha, and Yggdrasil are a couple of examples, but they all point to the Tree of Life. It is said to be wider than the eye could see and filled with rich foliage of too much to name. This tree had created the gods of good, and they, too, have many names. With their nurture and care, a world was born. First, the humans came with their high intelligence and creativity. As their imaginations grew, the people themselves created a world of myths and legends that all came true that the Tree of Life made happen. Soon, the humans shared a world with fairies, dragons, and other magical beings known as the mystics. Together, they helped each other make the planet earth what it was: a peaceful and beautiful world full of life, enchantment, and joy.

That bliss was short-lived as an evil and demonic entity swept through the earth like a shadow and began to manipulate the humans. Many of them started wars with themselves, and the mystics, and destroyed much of what they had created. This angered the gods, and they began to fear what human nature can do to the rest of the planet. The gods made things harder for humans by violent storms to terrible diseases. When things go from bad to worse, the tree begins to speak in all the hearts of the mortals and immortals.

"STOP IT!" It screamed as it lifted its roots, and its trunk gave off a bright, blinding light that showed off its very essence and power. After witnessing this wondrous sight, everyone, mortal and otherwise, obeyed the great tree. Once again, they faced the tree and began to listen to its words.

"Hear me now, for the truth is not to be forgotten. What was once can be again. This dark and evil time is not forever. I have seen the future, and one-day things will be better than ever. The human race has such potential to evolve, as do the rest of us. I have learned and grown just as the rest of you will."

The tree gave hope to all of those suffering from their own actions and wrongdoing to others. It also made a decision that day to create separate worlds for the mystics and humans, the Nether Realm and Earth Realm. For a time, things were peaceful once again for the mystics, and as the Tree of Life prophesied, humans began to learn and evolve. Soon, the Nether Realm became a myth, dismissed as a fairy tale and then was forgotten.

However, the Earth Realm was still a place that mystics loved to visit and enjoyed from time to time while it was home to humans. Portals would open where the mystics came and went as they pleased, but humans could never go into the Nether Realm unless it was in dreams, drugs, or insanity. Some humans, however, did manage to come and live in this world without resorting to such measures. The rare humans that accomplished this would have changed the world in a way that was positive to both realms. These amazing humans would "vanish into thin air", according to human records. It was not a curse but a gift, and most were never able to come back unless they chose to go by reincarnation and forget what they had seen in the Nether Realm.

They could not even go through the portals that are known to show up a time or two. The portals can never be controlled or used by humans. Portals are unpredictable, and they open by accident from time to time. Some portals are easy to close (like a haunted house), while others (like the Bermuda Triangle) could never be closed by the means of mankind.

Still, both worlds lived on and continued to dream of big things, but evil beings still caused chaos in both of these worlds. The malevolent entities didn't want either side to have peace or to evolve. They want to crush the good that both worlds have and continue to keep both worlds separate, if not in ruins. But time passes like the flow of the river, and the creatures in both worlds do not know if history is going to repeat itself all over again.

Chapter One

Merkiva, the market town of the Nether Realm. Where merchants and traders come a-wheeling-and-a-dealing, hoping to earn a fortune and eat like royalty while the customers come to see what's new in this hip and happening town, most of the shops are small one-storey fairy-tale cottages complete with straw roofs and stained-glass windows. There are a few rare stores that are made of grey stone or two-storey castle-like turrets. With these stores, people often lived in them as well as ran their businesses through them. Other smaller businesses are sold on blankets on the ground or in tents.

In Merkiva, there is always something original and different to see, from new foods to entertainers. It is a town that prides itself on being made of magic. Speaking of magic, there is a shop that in the center of town that is the talk of many far and wide. Trees cushion the small cottage that is known only as the "Nether Realm Magic Shop." There is always a new-fangled item that is beautiful, needful, and effective. The window display has an impressive and dramatic scene lying upon it. Delicate and vibrant blue velvet drapes over various heights and depths to resemble a bright, heavenly sky. On it are crystals of various colors, sizes, and shapes that sparkle in the sun. Behind it are some books that give some insight into what the store itself has and a small tree in the center of it all. Hanging in the windows are faceted dropped sun-catchers that make the shop look like a flow of rainbows.

On the wooden display shelves against the walls are dainty little glass bottles filled with various colored liquids of herbal bath and body products that do everything from energizing to relaxing the senses. Beside them are tiny dark bottles of aromatherapy that are used for just about everything.

There are more herbs that are packaged for culinary uses, teas, and potpourirs. Candles in bright colors bring on what they are labeled as. Beside them are nature products such as shells, glass flowers, and little trees. There is striking jewelry to be had in the display glass on the counter. Some of the jewelry has bright gleaming jewels, while others have interesting engravings, but all of them sparkle with the magic infused in them. Artwork, paintings, sculptures, and statues are displayed everywhere of various mythical creatures that give off the feeling of being in an art gallery. An antique book and crystal ball show themselves off, along with a golden antique cash register on a long wooden counter.

Whatever enchanted object is needed at the time is there in the "Nether Realm Magic Shop." By the window, behind the counter, stands a young nymph named Elfina, who is the shop's owner and keeper. Her bright green eyes watch the rain fall with child-like wonder despite the fact that it slows down her business. When she is lucky enough to feel the drops of water on her skin, she spins circles to feel the joy of it. To her, the rain washes away all the bad and brings on the better. Nature's own cleaning crew. A happy sigh escapes her sweet pink smile as she stands there barefoot with her toes painted a bright red this week. She pulls a hand through her softly wavy blonde hair that reaches all the way to her waist.

This is the kind of day I needed. Elfina thinks to herself as she smooths out her simple blue dress with its green leaves and white flowers patterning it. She remembers shopping with Jacqueline, who picked out this dress for her because it showed her bust nicely and a little leg from the knees.

Jacqueline always says that "appearances make the woman," to which Elfina agrees with her on that.

Keeping that in mind, Elfina looks into a small table mirror with thick gold ivy embroidery to check her makeup. The pixie salesgirl who sold her the cosmetics was right about the eyeshadow. The stardust sparkling silver is the perfect compliment to her light, fair skin.

A nice light flirtatiousness and sparkle on the eyes that brought out her inner goddess. As fun-looking as it is simple to put on. Throughout her whole life, Elfina never thinks of all the fussy little details that come with everyday life. She, like the rest of her fellow nymphs, just wanted to enjoy her life and not worry about the little things because it was a waste of time.

Elfina wonders what all her best friends are doing on a day like today. Jacqueline is probably enjoying it from her tower room as she would paint something gloomy while her husband is out and about fixing something. Rainy days are as inspiring to Jacqueline as it is to her. That and making love to her husband. It isn't surprising to her or any of their mutual friends that Jacqueline finds beauty in darkness. She is a vampire and has been for over 500 years. The stereotype of vampires is to be morose and melancholy, but despite this, Jacqueline is always fun and great to be around. This is thanks to her consistently glowing smile and infectious laugh.

The same goes for her husband of 300 years. Stephan, a werewolf who is a great contrast to her black cladded outfits and perfect manners with his plaid shirts, blue jeans, and the way he relaxes so easily wherever he plants himself.

Viola is a woman of the siren clan who lives in the seas with other mer-people like herself. She is a busy woman who works as a banker and yet always manages to come to the surface to see the rest of her friends. The sweet, shy, and quietly strong-willed Viola has a blush ready for any adult situation, which includes meeting someone new. However, she is never afraid to go after what she wants. Which right now includes that job promotion to bank manager. She is a woman determined to make her own way in life, in and out of the water. She is (no doubt) at work right now, busting her tail, but she did promise to come out tonight despite the rain. It takes time for her tail to dry and change into legs, but that never stops her.

Then there is the practical, no-nonsense elf-maiden Meira, who works as a sword and shield creator and repairer. She knows everything there is to know about being a blacksmith. Her boyfriend, Osmond (Ozzie for short), who is also an elf, takes care of the business end of their shop. It is charming to see them both together in and out of the shop.

The way he would sit up at the front of the counter or do the ledgers, and she would be in the back of the smithery, creating one of her masterpieces.

The way the two of them would pass each other the instruments of their choices is a romance novel on its own. Meira would hand him a pen, and Ozzie would hand her a hammer. Then, a smile is given on both sides as Meira leans forward and kisses him sweetly. The romantic affection between the two of them has the whole group constantly wondering when they actually are going to get married. The ladies all had a pool of when that was going to be. By Viola's logical guesstimate, they will be married in 30 years, while the more experienced Jacqueline thinks it will be another 50 years. The ever-romantic Elfina believes that it will be in 25 years.

When Meira found out about this pool, the three of them thought she would be angry. Instead, she put down her share of money and suggested 45 years. A great sense of humour mixed with a good nature and a dry, sarcastic wit gives you one person: Meira. She rounds the group off with practical advice and a cynical remark or two.

Such as the other day when she remarked about Elfina's penchant to go barefoot. "You wear your bare feet so much that you are going to get troll's feet one day."

And what did Elfina do? Stick her tongue out at her, of course.

Elfina is not close to her parents, but she does have a family with her three best friends and their respective spouses. Her life is full as she has her own business that she has had an undeniable success of for over 100 years. She travels everywhere to see everything that the Nether Realm has to offer, which is a lot. A beautiful home in the rainbow-esque forest to keep an eye on her kind but absentminded guardian named Javas.

And then there is Iris, her own loveable friend, business partner, and cat. Right now, she is rubbing her long body against Elfina's bare legs. Elfina picks Iris up and holds her close to stroke her lovely soft gray fur. She is a lucky nymph indeed and plans to stay that way.

"Alright, you miserable blockheads!" Yells the booming voice of Tomnock Cree that, snaps Elfina out of her gratitude meditation.

Elfina turns and smiles at the red-faced, long-bearded dwarf waving his arm in a manic circle. She gently places Iris down on the floor and turns to look at the six small men handling a large wooden box. She turns her gaze to Tommy Cree, who is the shipment manager of the "Underground Shipment Inc." Four feet tall and touchier than a mean-spirited phoenix, he works his employees hard, but he rewards them well.

"Get that shipment in here!" He bellows. "Damn leeches, that's what I waste my precious gold on you for!"

Elfina doesn't bother to hide her chuckle as he comes up to her counter on the small set of steps. "Hi, Tommy."

"Hello, Elfina." He replies in a boisterous but friendly manner. "Fine-looking weather we are having today."

"It sure is. That's why I thought you and your boys would love to lug something heavy here today."

"Naturally." Tommy sighs in pure pleasure at being covered in cold water and mud. "It helps to cool us down."

"So, how are things? Would you like some tea?" Elfina asks as she leans on her counter.

"Nah!" He shakes his head at her offer. "I'm switching back to coffee."

"So that is why you are in such a good mood today." She impishly blinks at him.

"Hey! Delivering a shipment to not only a beautiful client but my favorite client is all I need," Tommy says, matching his playful look to hers.

Elfina stirs her head. The dwarves begin to open up the crate with a crowbar after hearing them pound harshly into the giant box. Tommy turns to his crew and stomps off the steps. She watches his approachable face instantly morph into an aggravated one.

"What the hell do you think you're doing? Be careful there!" He yells as he walks over to the crate and takes the crowbar from one of the other dwarves. "There are valuables in there! Get your head out of your ass and pay attention!"

After getting the other dwarves to move aside, Tommy demonstrates how it is "supposed" to be done.

Elfina does her best to try and hide her giggle as she watches Tommy get his dander up. The other dwarves stood in a half circle, watching Tommy with amusement. It looks like they, too, could not help but find this situation funny. With the crowbar lodged in, Tommy pulls against it, and a loud snap vibrates in the store.

"Gently open it, you wet-brained-apes!" With that, Tommy returns to Elfina's counter, where she is still standing and watching the action unfold.

The rest of the dwarves shake their heads, enjoying themselves before getting back to the job at hand. They all know that Tommy is all bark and no bite. He just believes in working hard even when he doesn't have to.

"How's your family doing, Tommy? Got any new pictures?" Elfina inquires, knowing just how to bring the softie out of him.

A gushy smile spreads on his face as he pulls out a small portrait of his wife and newborn son. "Look! Look! He finally has a smile." Elfina looks at the picture, seeing the small baby being wrapped around his mother's arms, beaming. "Now the wife says he has her smile, but you and I know better."

With a look of pure happiness on his face, Elfina feels the kindness and love radiate from him. She could tell that everything he did, he did for them. Now, being the savvy businesswoman that she is, Elfina takes this opportunity to make an observation not just for her but for his employees, too.

"Your boys seem a little strained, Tommy."

"Yeah." He utters, hunching his shoulders forward and putting a hand on his lower back. "We've been so busy lugging this and that everywhere that our backs have been giving us some trouble."

Elfina takes this statement as her cue and walks over to one of her shelves. She picks up a medium, stout green bottle along with a couple of stems of bark from the clear glass jar beside it. It's a good thing she stocked up on her inventory that day. For the past week, it's been all about back pain and muscle spasms that her customers have been coming in with. She turns to look at all of the men and can tell right away what they are in desperate need of.

Elfina walks over to Tommy, hands him the bottle, and puts the bark in a plastic bag for him. "Here you are, Tommy. This should help you guys out."

"Thanks, Elfie." He takes the bottle and the bag to examine them both. "But what is it? What do you do with it?"

"In the bottle is cayenne pepper and Saint John's wort mixed with Jack Frost oil. You put this on your lower back. It will have a warming effect at first, but with the oil, it will cool down to your skin and relieve the pain." Elfina explains and then points to the bag of bark. "This is willow bark. You guys need to chew on that in order to feel better from the inside out. After a decent night's rest, your backs should be better in a day or so."

"Perfect! Thanks, Elfina." He speaks as he puts the items in his brown satchel. "What do I owe you?"

"The shipment?" Elfina bats her eyelashes mischievously at him for a second time.

"Nice try, Sweetheart! What else you got?" He grins and wiggles his fingers at her.

Elfina sighs, knowing that she can't trick him, so she tells him the truth. "The combined two is worth 50 GPs or one translucent gem."

Tommy pulls out the invoice from his satchel and looks over to her. "Alright, well, our service is 200 GPs or 4 TGs. With this new deal, it will be 150 GPs or 3 TGs."

After hearing this, Elfina takes out a deep-blue velvet bag full of gold pieces and gives it to him. With a twinkle in his eye, Tommy takes the bag. Elfina expected to get this deal from him. She may have had a small dose of clairvoyance that all nymphs had, but she prefers to use her good people skills to make business deals happen. Besides, to her mind, battering can bring a better deal, especially when she gets a new supplier, friend, or a valuable item. If it is a new item, she could always keep it for herself or charge it up with magic and sell it to someone else.

"Great honey, I'll see you again." Tommy puts the pouch in his bag and walks off the steps.

"I hope so." Elfina coyly winks at him.

"Sly flirt." He replies as he walks over towards his crew, who are just starting to walk out the door. All of them are eyeing Tommy with delight as they go. "Alright, shows over you tiny-brained pukes! Get moving!" Elfina wobbles her head and grabs her tiny dust pan with a brush. Just as Tommy stops at the door, he turns and speaks. "You'll save me a dance for the Centennial World Celebration, right?"

"For you Tommy, you can have as many dances as you wish." With an affectionate smile on both parts, Tommy leaves and Elfina goes to tidy up her shop. She had made some pretty good sales today and thinks she should close the shop early. A knowing smirk appears on her face as she puts her broom and dustpan back under her counter. She still has to put her new shipment in the back room. So, she walks over to the newly opened crate and gathers all the jewels inside.

Perhaps she will drop in on Meira and see if she can get her to close her shop early too. It is Saturday after all. That means that it is ladies' night with her friends. Elfina looks forwards to this every week when she and her friends get together at the pub or wherever the group's mood is. There are times when they have dinner or lunch together when it isn't Saturday, but ladies' night is their sacred get-together.

After she slips on her silver shoes, Elfina turns the open sign to closed. Iris, being the independent cat that she is, goes to her bed behind the counter and falls asleep. Elfina had already taken out a piece of fish for her and made sure she had enough water for the night. With a spring in her step, Elfina puts on her shawl, locks her doors, and leaves the store for the night.

As she walks, Elfina beholds all the shops, tents, and outdoor kiosks. Maya, the psychic, seems to be doing well with the long line-up of clients waiting by her tent. They don't seem to be bothered by the increment weather as they all just sit around on chairs or stand in the rain awaiting to be called inside.

Maya steps outside of the tent and calls out, "Burdock! You're next, dear."

That is when the stony golem stands up from the chair, and Maya holds the tent door flap open for him. As he steps inside, Elfina sends a wave to Maya, and she returns it with a nod. She brushes a heavy ringed hand through her black curled hair with a silver streak before straightening out her shining purple paisley skirt.

Elfina could not help but admire Maya. She is an elegant and intelligent woman who uses her integrity and gifts to help others. Elfina remembers how she came into her store one day looking for tarot cards that truly "speak" to her. Luckily, not only did she find that, but a bright blue crystal that matched her eyes to a tee. Many gypsies believed that when a crystal ball matches your eyes, you see all of the destiny unfold. Since then, she has used both divination tools to lead others to better lives.

Elfina walks on and sees the giant Persian rug where the "Dancing Trifle Triplets" are putting on their latest performance. Under their magical dome that they had summoned to block the rain, they dance a sensual routine where they wave their hips and reach their arms out like they are swimming. Elfina stops to watch with the small crowd gathering around them.

It is hard to believe that the three of them are sisters. They all look so different. Although they were all slender, one sister had blue eyes and blonde hair, another had red hair and green eyes, and the last one had black hair and violet eyes. Today, the three of them are wearing identical black belly-dancing outfits, tantalizing and teasing the crowd with their exotic dance. The three of them line up in a straight line and let out a big clap, putting their hands together.

As the crowd cheers them on, the raven-haired triplet comes forward and summons up a magical scroll with a red enchanted quill. It hovers in the air as she begins to speak. "If you liked what you saw today, just know that you can learn our magical dance. Sign up today on our scroll and get a 20% off discount."

Elfina watches a few people go towards the scroll to sign their names. Elfina doesn't join them. She loves dancing, but to her, it is about celebrations, not shows.

Next to the triplet's tent is Meira's home and weapons shop. Elfina treads into the shop, which is filled with lanterns on the ceilings and swords, and shields adorning the walls. A long wooden counter sits in the back of the store. From the back door behind the counter comes Meira with her shoulder-length brown hair tied back in a leather thong. Her brown, elvish face is covered with dirt and sweat from hard labour. A smile appears on her face when she sees Elfina. Dirty or clean, Meira always glows, especially with that smile.

"Hi, Sweetheart!" She greets her friend with a hug. "You're here early."

"Yes. It was a little slow in my shop today, but I had a steady stream of customers in the morning."

Meira turns the open sign to closed. "Yes. The same thing happened here, so I decided to fix up this beauty." She walks into her workshop at the back of the store and brings back a 6-foot-tall spear with a silver pole and some unique designs on the spearhead.

"Wow!" Elfina says as Meira hands her the weapon, "This magnificent Meira. Whose spear is this?"

"Mine," Meira answers smugly. "I bought it a week ago and have been really fixing it up."

Elfina hands the spear back to her and walks with Meira to her workshop. It is dark and full of clutter. The room is filled with the instruments and tools of metal molding, complete with an anvil in the center of the room. Meira hangs the spear back on her shelf and gestures to Elfina to come up with her to the apartment.

The apartment is sedate and humble, which is how both Meira and Ozzie prefer it. They don't believe in decoration or impractical objects. "If you didn't use it, you didn't need it." That is their motto. On the light purple couch sits Meira's lover and business partner, Ozzie, with a glass of red wine in one hand, a pen in the other, and a burgundy ledger on his lap. His bald head shines despite the lack of sun, while his amber eyes are skimming the figures of the day. His thin mouth has a half smile, lifting his high cheekbones ever-so-slightly with it. By the content expression on his pale, light-colored face, the store has broken even today.

"Hi, Ozzie!" Elfina sends him a gracious wave and smile. "How're things?"

He looks up at her and returns the smile. "Oh great. Stephan and I are going to Colusa to watch the fight."

"Oh, right! Who's fighting again?"

17

"The Amazon Meg against Rand the Barbarian." He toasts his glass to her.

"Right." Elfina nods, "I hear it's supposed to be a hell of a fight."

"Yeah." Ozzie raises his eyebrows in anticipation and finishes the last of his wine. "A damn good fight."

They both laugh with one another before Elfina follows Meira into her bedroom through an archway. Meira goes into her bathroom to shower the dirt and sweat from her body while Elfina goes into her bedroom closet to help pick out a clean outfit. When Meira comes back into the bedroom, she realizes something.

"Oh! How is Viola going to get here if it's raining?" Meira asks as she slips on her long brown pants. Elfina holds up two different shirts for her to choose from.

"Jacqueline is picking her up in her coach by that small cave that Viola waits in."

"Phew! That's one worry off my mind." Meira nods as she picks out the long-sleeved shirt of two different shades of blue. "Do you think it will stop raining by then?"

With a shrewd snicker that they both give each other, the two of them start laughing. They both know that the rain won't stop yet. As both races of elves and nymphs are attuned to nature, they can sense what the weather is going to be for days at a time. After Meira readies herself, they walk into the hall.

"Bye, Ozzie!" The two women unitedly say and chuckle as they leave.

Ozzie smiles and waves goodbye to them as they head down the stairs.

"Did you hear about Lady Merida?" Meira questions, looking over to Elfina with great concern in her eyes as they walk out of the store.

"No. Did something happen?" Elfina probes, matching her friend's worried look with a curious expression. Meira accounts the story to Elfina.

Chapter Two

Lady Merida was having a party in her large luxurious mansion. She was an angel in every sense of the word and takes this role very seriously. She was known to have the most vibrant and entertaining parties in all of the Nether Realm. If a person is lucky enough to be invited, which can take a long time due to the lengthy waitlist, they are guaranteed the best night ever. Anyone and everyone was invited, no matter their standings or fame.

To that end, at her parties, she asks for gold pieces or gem donations. These donations go to various charities in need of miracles in the Earth Realm. A single miracle can cost a lot of gold and gems. This was why Lady Merida does everything in her power to make sure that these humans, animals, etc., get as many miracles as she can muster. Every angel has a duty to create as many miracles for others as possible. In this case, throwing opulent soirees is hers.

The night was like any other. The theme of the party this time was "Masquerade Ball." As one could see, thanks to the large banner over the giant double doors entering her house announcing it. Lady Merida was making her rounds in the ballroom, floating gracefully from guest to guest. She is dressed elegantly in a gold bodice and matching skirt with a glittering white mask adorned with golden feathers. Her dark hair was swept up in a stylish French twist, and her ebony-colored skin glowed like diamond dust.

She reviewed her party with an observant eye. By the look on all of her guests' smiling faces, they are having a marvelous time. She had personally made sure that the food and wine were above and beyond. Each delicate canape and finger food that she had selected was considered with great care. It was meant to lull the people into heavenly eustasy. Then, the lively red wine mix she had brought in was tested by one of the Earth Realm's most respected sommeliers. For that reason, she knew that it was one of the best.

The music that was floating in the atmosphere spoke of good times and merriment. Each guest was dancing up a joyful storm on the ballroom floor. She looked over to the musical instruments that were playing themselves. The bass stood up tall with each string being strummed at the precise time, the violin and its bow gave off a sweet twang, and the saxophone let out a jazzy tune. When these instruments played together, it brought the whole party together.

Lady Merida made her way to the charmed coin box that sat before the stage, allowing all the patrons to put in their donations. The box itself was an intricately decorated chest trimmed with gold and an elaborate lid that looked like two waves crashing into the ocean. Lady Merida took a white-gloved hand and stroked the box to get a sense of how many coins she had earned during the party. By her senses, she had already gained enough for at least three miracles, which will be delivered to the Children's Hospital ASAP.

Suddenly, she heard her doorbell chime with the musical "Halleluiah!" ringing out into the room. Clearly, she had one more guest, and the whole room noticed this. However, after the bell stopped ringing, the guests went back to their enjoyment of the party. Lady Merida made her way to the door to see who was there. When she opened the door, she got quite a surprise.

At the doorway was a 6-foot-tall dark stranger in a black fedora and leather trench coat. A person that she could not see any distinguishing features, but she figured that was because the entryway tends to be a little shadowy. That and there was an air of intimidation about this being. They bring up a mask decorated with black pearls and black glass jewels as if to show her.

"Party time." It said in an emotionless whisper.

Lady Merida smiled and stepped aside. "Come in!"

As the being passed her with an odd kind of grace that you would normally find a ghost having, Lady Merida felt a chill, but she could not turn someone away just because of a feeling. It's not in her character to be unnecessarily cruel. This being was probably just a little different, if not socially awkward. She shrugged her shoulders and told herself, "It happens." Besides, she has had plenty of ghosts at her parties.

*****

Hours later, Lady Merida was standing at her front door holding the donations box as each guest approached her. As they were leaving. The guests made sure they added some more gold pieces to her latest cause.

"Wonderful night, Darling!" Said the fox spirit that lifted her red mask with a wink and dropped a translucent gem into the donations box.

"Thank you for coming, Tashi." Lady Merida kissed both her cheeks as she left.

Then, a centaur in a blue tuxedo approached her. "Thanks again for the fabulous night. Your music is superb as always."

After dropping some more gold pieces into the box, Lady Merida grins at him. "Take care, Abas. I sense your farm is doing well?"

"Indeed. It's been a good year."

With a chuckle from Lady Merida, all of her guests have left, and her party is officially over. She walked back inside her house and into her ballroom towards the donation box's stand. She put the box on the stand and slowly opened it up. There were over a million gold pieces in there! Lady Merida was ecstatic to see this. Lots of miracles are going to that Children's hospital.

Suddenly, she heard a sound that was an eerie combination of a breath and a whisper. She spun around, not knowing where this sound came from. Her eyes searched every corner until they landed on the east balcony. There, she saw the mysterious dark guest that she had let in earlier looking down at her ominously.

"What are you doing up there?" she yelled up at the being. They said nothing. Instead, they form into a smoky mass that, in seconds, becomes a shapeless fog.

It was then she realized what was happening and what this being was. That stranger was a shadow person, a demon that she now had in her house. A person was to never let them in, but she did, and now she was in danger. At that moment, she slapped her own hand and scolded herself for being so stupid. In terror, she stepped backwards and ran into the donations box. It knocked over, and gold pieces spilled all over the floor.

Without even thinking about it, Lady Merida crouched down and gathered all the coins that spilled. She didn't care what this creature did, but she was not going to let it take away these children's miracles.

An evil laugh filled the ballroom as the shadow materialized on the ground floor behind the angel. Lady Merida cranked her neck and looked behind her to see that the demon had taken the shape of a man again. She had a sick, sinking feeling in her gut, but she refused to be scared of this evil shade. She turned and gathered the rest of the coins and put them back in the box.

After the last coin was in the box, she ran towards the back of the room. She knew the being was still standing behind her as she did not hear him step or transport himself. Angels always knew what was happening in their environment. It was a special form of power that they had. However, she did not predict that the demon would appear before her at the back door.

Holding the box close to her chest, Lady Merida's thoughts were of the children who needed these miracles, and this creature is not going to stop her from giving them that. Shadow demons are unpredictable. Sometimes they caused harm and sometimes they didn't but what they always want to do is stir up fear. Lady Merida would not allow that to happen. She turned to face the west wing only to bump into the demon's humanoid form. She puts a hand to its' chest and finds it solid as hard flesh.

"Let me by." She said in a fierce tone that had undercurrents of dread in it. "You won't have these miracles."

"I don't care about miracles." It said in its' guttural growl of a voice. It slammed its dark arm on the box and knocked it to the ground once more.

Lady Merida pulled her hand into a fist and charged all her light energy into it. She prepared to let it fire on this massive dark spirit. Unfortunately, it grabbed a hold of her fist before she could let the light ball fly. Gripping her arm tightly, it took its' other hand to grab her by her neck. She feels the icy chill of it like a bloodless zombie. She gasped for air when it lifted her off the ground like she was completely weightless. It lifted her high as she struggled to release herself.

Finally able to see its face, it had the visage of a deathly white emotionless face. Soon, its hollow black eyes and mouth dribbled a black liquid. Unable to scream, Lady Merida collapsed, and her glowing dark skin became cold and white. The demon drops her to the ground as a stone statue that all angels become when their time is done.

Little did they know that Ark the Giant had witnessed this horrible crime. He had forgotten his hat when he collected his jacket and had just wanted to pop in without bothering Lady Merida. Instead, he heard her scream and peered around the corner. He saw this shadow sucking the life right out of her. After the nightmare he just witnessed, Ark fled in terror to the closest Knights and Valkyrie's Quarters as fast as he could run.

*****

It was a routine night at the Knights and Valkyries Station. Sir Percival was sitting at the desk looking at the crystal ball, keeping apprised of what was happening out in the area. By the look of the bare crystal, there was nothing to report. He leaned up against his fist, thinking about what his brothers and sisters-in-arms were doing right now. Probably just as bored as he was, they get to patrol around, not sit in one place like he was. A sigh escaped his lips, and the crystal ball had no image in it whatsoever. That means there was nothing going on at all.

Just before he can nod off, Ark, the giant, bursts through the station's double doors.

"I'm awake! I'm awake!" Sir Percival said, startled, with his arms splayed across the counter. He looked up and saw Ark. It's a good thing the shrinking potion Ark used still worked; otherwise, he could take this whole place down. "Ark? What the hell is going on?!"

"It's Lady Merida!" He gushed out, huffing and puffing in panic. "She's been killed!"

"What?!" Sir Percival sat up straight and alert.

"It was a shadow demon!" He yelled. "It sucked the life right out of her."

Tears started overflowing out of Ark's eyes, finally coming to terms with what he had just seen. One of the Nether Realm's most famous socialites and beloved angels was murdered right in front of him. He buried his bearded face into his hands and began to tremble. Sobs escaped from the normally big man, and he grew pale. Sir Percival ran around the counter and led Ark to one of the waiting chairs sitting against the wall.

"Here, Ark." He calmly responded to the hyperventilating man by patting his back. "Listen. Breathe. I'll send out a squad right now,, but I need you to calm down. Remember, if you vomit or even cry out too much, you will go from being 6'4 back to 11 feet. That would be bad."

Ark slowed his breathing and wiped his eyes dry as he knew that the Knight was speaking the truth. He slowly calmed down and looked to Sir Percival.

"I'll call the other Knights and Valkyries immediately." Sir Percival announced. "Then, if you are able, can I take you into my office and get your statement?"

A teary-eyed Ark nodded at him and stood up. The Knight put a comforting hand on his shoulder and led him towards his office. As

25

they passed the counter, Sir Percival tapped on an intricate silver bell that called the nearest protectors to the station. Quickly, he turned back towards Ark.

*****

Without a moment to lose, the Knights raced on their enchantedly enhanced horses at great speed, with the Valkyries taking the sky on their winged horses. The dispatch made its way to Lady Merida's mansion in a matter of seconds. A full sweep needed to be done before the psychics and healers could be brought in.

It was the Knights and Valkyries' job to help the victims, find the villains, and secure the area. As always, they were the first ones on the scene to make sure that everything was safe for an investigation to take place.

The men and women parked their assigned horses to the side of the front stairwell. Carefully, all of the protectors hold their shields in front of them and unsheathe their weapons. Some of them have swords, while others have spears. Slowly, they marched up the stairs and opened the grand double entrance doors. In their fastest sprints, the guardians spread out throughout the house.

They barged into every room to find no sign of the shadow demon. However, when they looked into the ballroom, they saw the stone-statued remains of Lady Merida. Knowing that when an angel is killed, they are turned into stone, the Knights and Valkyries remove their helmets out of respect. There she was with her face turned to the sky and twisted in an agonized scream as if she had suffered an enormous amount of pain.

"We have to catch this bastard." The platinum-haired Valkyrie stated to the red-headed Knight beside her.

He could not help but agree and nodded his head at her. The Knights and Valkyries stood there staring at the angel's statue, waiting for the psychics and healers to come. They could not wait to get to the bottom of this horrible offense. The thought that this gracious woman being murdered filled them all with anger. Who that hell deserves a death like this, let alone an angel?

*****

"That really happened?" Elfina asks Meira with her eyes wide in astonishment.

"Yes, it did."

"Well, at least Ark did the right thing by going to the Knights and Valkyries."

"That's not all he did either. The next day, he told everyone he knew about it and printed a news article about what happened." Meira explains. "He warned everyone. So, we best keep our guard up about this. Who knows what will happen?"

Elfina feels a chill going up her arms, and not just because of the rain. Creepy demons running around isn't exactly her idea of a good time. She looks ahead to see the pub they are going to and silently hopes that this situation is being taken care of. With a shake of her body, Elfina forces the bad vibes she is getting out of her, and the two of them walk inside the Black Dragon Pub.

The Black Dragon Pub, despite its harsh name, is a warm and inviting place to spend a good evening with some friends. The open spaces, its cabin-like atmosphere are what make this place like a second home to Elfina and all of her friends. Colorful, glowing paper lanterns are strung up high across the ceiling to bring in some vivacity. The rainbow of candles that sits on each table shows that the owners know how to practice a little color magic.

Elfina looks at the patio, which is empty right now, but remembers that it is the best place for a romantic date. The outside has flowers on every table, a tiered fountain in the center, and exotic botanicals in baskets adorning the walls and ground. The tea candles out there will float in mid-air and are charmed to avoid all customers when they draw near for their own safety. To Elfina, this is the place to have a hot date.

27

The owner of this marvelous establishment is a rogue wizard named Viktor. Rogue means that he did not follow what is considered standard wizardry rules. Instead of being a teacher, scholar, or magician and wearing the suitable wizard attire of robes, he likes to wear vintage Armani suits from the Earth Realm and chooses to serve cocktails and comfort food. Unlike many of his predecessors, Viktor is a social man who loves good company and Earth Realm's top-40 music. Despite his unconventional ways, Viktor still has the long white beard and hair to match, his kind face always had a smile on it that lights up a room (literally, it's how he lights the candles), and his bright, vibrant blue eyes always have a mischievous sparkle to them. It's like he has a secret that he refuses to tell anyone.

Tonight, he is working at the bar in the far-left corner of the pub with his sleeves rolled up and mixing drinks with various floating tools. The shaker is shaking above his head, the mixer floating to his left is mixing an opaque concoction, and a bottle of clear liquid is being poured into a martini glass. Viktor himself is wiping down a beer mug with his bare hands. Elfina silently wonders why he didn't just charm that as well, but it could be because he had enough on the go. Looking around the pub, it is clearly full tonight.

Servers are scurrying in many random directions, carrying trays of food and drinks or taking away the dirty dishes. The female servers were adorned head-to-toe in their uniforms of corsets, white peasant tops, and rainbow-colored skirts, while the males had colorful vests and brown pantaloons. The busty brunette server with sweet brown eyes and a tattoo heart on her chest walks over to Elfina and Meira with a friendly smile on her cherry-red lips.

"Hi, ladies! Good to see you, again." She says in her usual cheery self.

"Hi, Cyllene." Elfina returns the gracious greeting with a beam of her own. "Busy tonight?"

Cyllene grabs the menus and replies, "Little bit. I blame the weather. What about you?"

"Well, a little slow, but it happens whenever we get a downpour like this." Elfina casually responds. "How's Yew Mountain?"

"Lovely as usual." Cyllene lets out a happy exhale. "Come with me, girls."

While they follow Cyllene, Elfina recollects her fellow nymph's life. She is an Oread who lives up in the Yew Mountains with a lot of birds and mountain goats to keep her company. It has a large waterfall and enough plant life to make it a perfect home for any nymph. What makes it so unique is the various crystals that sparkle and shine everywhere a person would look. Although it is near the desert, Cyllene is a swift, expert hiker and always makes it to her shift on time.

She loves working at the Black Dragon. Always wearing the best hair and make-up combination, which is not cheap, Cyllene lives her best life thanks to working there. At the end of every shift, she first grabs the best bottle of wine, buys it, and takes it home with her. Usually, she is not alone when she does leave. As a confident and strong woman, she has a healthy sexual appetite and doesn't care who knows about it. Then again, no one really thinks much of it, either.

After they finally get to their seats, Viktor himself walks over carrying two glasses with pewter accents containing the two women's drinks of choice. "Hello, my favorite beauties." He chimes as he sets down the glasses. "How's business today?"

"Great!" The two of them say unanimously and giggle.

Letting out a chuckle himself, Viktor also asks. "Are the rest of the musketeers coming today?"

"Yes, sir, and we are all starving. I promise you this." Meira says, looking at her menu.

"Will they be having their usuals too?"

"Viola, yes, but if you want to really impress Jacqueline, get her a clam and tomato juice," Elfina answers playfully.

"She's not on a diet again, is she?" Meira smirks, but Elfina can hear the slight bit of anxiety in her voice.

"Yep." Elfina breathes out and grabs her wine glass. "Let's hope she isn't too grouchy today."

Of course, after she says this, both Jacqueline and Viola walk into the pub. Or, in this case, Jacqueline carrying a tarp-wrapped Viola into the pub to keep her legs from turning back into a fishtail. As Elfina waves them over, she once again marvels at the inhuman strength that Jacqueline possesses, especially wearing those deadly stiletto heels. Still, everyone is grateful that she has this gift at times like this. It is much easier for Viola to get around on the surface when the atmosphere is against them. Jacqueline walks over to the table with Viola still in her arms.

"Did you two just get married?" Meira sarcastically chuckles as she raises her glass of beer to them Jacqueline sets Viola on the chair beside her.

"Sorry, honey. I'm taken already." Jacqueline laughs, holding up her engagement and wedding rings to show off to Meira as she sits in the chair beside Elfina. "Besides, I don't think my husband would like to know I got married to Viola."

Both Elfina and Meira snort as the other two ladies roll their eyes at each other. Viola pushes the plastic tarp off of her newly morphed legs. Viktor comes over at the right time with Jacqueline's clam/tomato juice and Viola's glass of white wine.

"I think he would understand, wouldn't he?" Meira pipes up as she takes a swig of her beer. "I mean, vampires are bisexual, aren't they?"

Jaqueline tosses her long, wavy red hair and answers, "More like pansexual. And yes, he was really excited when I told him I had a fling with Valerie and her now lover, Willa. But that didn't work out so well for me, like it does for some vamps."

"But you love being married to Stephan, don't you?" Elfina inquires, giving Jacqueline that starry-eyed look she gets when talking about romance.

Jacqueline's fangs begin to surface as she picks up her drink. "Oh yes. Married 300 years and still smoking hot despite being dead first."

"I thought it was undead, Love." Meira archly corrects Jacqueline.

"How could I forget?" Jacqueline says as she pulls down her sparkling black scarf to reveal the bite marks on her neck. With a laugh going around their little circle, Viola pipes up.

"Well, at least you wake up fully aware, have easy dinner planning, and get the added bonus of an orgy at the end of the day." Everyone turns and looks at Viola in shock. The three of them could not contain their laughter from bursting out. The fact that Viola even mutters the word "orgy" is a huge surprise, especially when she blushes every time the topic of sex is brought up.

"Isn't that my line?" Jacqueline funs.

"And isn't that more Elfina's thing?" Meira asks, looking at Elfina with an impish smile. "Awareness, food, and orgies?"

A huge hoot erupts as Elfina begins to explain. "Now that's the common misconception of nymphs, especially with what humans seem to think."

"Why is that?" Viola asks with a combination of sincere curiosity and unapologetic amusement.

"Because, my dear, Viola," Elfina lectures joyfully doing her best impersonation of a distinguished university professor, but then switches back to her normal voice. "That idiot Pan thought that we were worth playing with just because we are innocent, unselfconscious, and don't believe in restrictions. Then some philosopher got the wrong idea, and we got a bad rep ever since."

"Yuck! Him?" Viola asks with genuine disgust scrunching on her face.

Elfina merely nods before Meira asks, "Is he still chasing you, Elfina?"

"Yes." She answers aggravatedly looking up to the ceiling. "The last time I saw him was two days ago when he glamoured himself into a clean-cut, handsome chocolate salesman and tried to come into my house while I was reading my tarot cards."

"So, what happened?" Jaqueline inquires in her saucy slinky manner. "Did you kill him?"

"Tempting, but no. I leave that up to you." Elfina retorts her friend's sass while patting her hand. "But what I did do was have some vines grow up from my stoop and cover those cloven legs of his. Of course, he freaked out, screaming, "Snakes! Snakes!" and he fell. He landed ass first on one of my healing stones."

They all laugh out loud as Elfina continues her story. "That thing was shoved so far up there that he glamoured back into himself and made an emergency visit to the proctologist!"

They all nearly fall over laughing at her story. Elfina is not a promiscuous woman; she is the kind of nymph who chooses to give herself to a man with careful consideration. Pan is a creature who will never be worthy of such pleasure from her. To her and the rest of the nymphs, Pan has been dubbed a laughingstock since Selene dumped him after their tryst.

When Selene had overheard his plan for his next conquest of another minor goddess, she made him impotent for 150 years. Not only that, she left him dangling on the cliffs with the sheep's skin he wrapped himself with. When he was there, he blubbered like the useless little cretin that he was and admitted that he loved using people. After that,

Selene told Artemis, and Artemis had told every other woman about him. He hasn't had any tail since.

After the four of them had ordered their food, they continued with their conversation.

"Maybe he'll learn now." Viola cheerfully chirps up.

"Yeah, right," Meira says raising an eyebrow and having another sip of her beer. "And I think you are right about that, Elfina. I've never seen much of your kind do anything but flirt and dance around naked. Nothing necessarily to do with sex."

"We know she does." Jacqueline chuckles, pointing her thumb to Elfina, and sips her special juice. "But do the rest of the nymphs? That is the question."

"Don't know, really," Meira says. "I can't really speak for my close elf cousins."

"Why? Are elves easy, Meira?" Elfina asks with a mischievous mask, hiding her curiosity.

She pretends to think very hard about those questions as she exaggeratedly flips her head from side to side and taps her chin. "We do enjoy it, and most of us aren't virgins, but like everything else we do, we tend to do it with care and wisdom."

"That makes me hot just thinking about it, Meira," Jacqueline tosses a playfully smoldering look at Meira while straightening out her low-cut, black sparkled gown. "I should marry you."

"Ah!" Meira waves a hand at her and takes another drink of her beer, "Save it for your husband, but I guess you don't need it with that handsome bloke! Besides, you're not my type. To ride this ride, you need a penis."

Viola blushes profusely, shakes her head, and covers her face as she laughs. "You ladies are despicable!"

"Spoken by the one who brought up orgies in the first place," Meira says as they all continue to laugh.

When the food finally comes around, Viola eats a piece of shrimp, Meira talks about the weather, and Elfina pretends to listen as she eats a carrot from her vegetable plate. She can't shake off her concern when Meira mentions what happened to Lady Merida. Jacqueline looks over at her and can sense that something is on Elfina's mind. Elfina knows that her vampiric friend can read her mind and doesn't bother hiding it. Jacqueline does respect her friends' privacy, but when she feels concerned or knows that one of the people that she loves is unhappy, she has to do something about it.

"What's going on in there, Elfina?" Meira asks as she looks over to her friend, matching Jacqueline's concern. "It's not about that jerk, Pan, is it?"

Elfina smiles, feeling a bit embarrassed and confesses. "No, it's about Lady Merida."

"I've heard about that!" Viola states. "Has anyone found the demon that killed her yet?"

"No." Jacqueline shakes her head at her. "The authorities don't know exactly how this creature killed her. In the paper today, Ark said that it looked like the life was being sucked out of her, but he didn't see how it did it. No incantations, no wounds of any kind, just nothing."

"She was such a good woman," Elfina says, feeling a little blue, until Jacqueline puts a comforting black-gloved hand on her bare hand. "She was not only a good woman and a great party planner, but she did great things. It's always upsetting when an angel is killed."

"Who didn't love her parties?" Meira asks. "Every time we go to another party, we shall all remember her fondly and party hard for her."

"Hear hear." Viola toasts her white wine in the air, and the rest of the friends raise their glasses to hers in honor of their favorite angel.

"Cheers ladies," Meira says with a wide smile. "Here's to the most wonderful angel we knew that threw the best parties for charity."

"Yes." All the ladies say, toasting their glasses.

Chapter Three

Lady Merida's funeral was quite the ceremony to be had. It was also touching to see how many people loved her from her admirers, to her friends and to her suitors. It was held at her manor which seemed appropriate due to her statued-self still lingering there. The room was adorned with all of her favorite flowers which were lilies and camellias, sitting prettily in the scattered vases. People were sitting in rows while the priest stood beside her, sharing his kind words. Looking at her longingly and lovingly.

Elfina, Jacqueline, Viola, and Meira were sitting on the chairs in the tenth row. The sadness of this tragedy weighed heavy in this room.

"You have touched all of our hearts, my lady." The priest on the stage said. "You certainly have touched mine."

After the priest had said his final words, he put a hand on Lady Merida's stony shoulder and let his tears fall before he turned to face the audience with a sad smile. "For our dear angel's departure, let's have this last party in her honor. Please fold your chairs and put them in the back of the room."

In minutes, the soiree was in full swing. The theme was "Garden Party," and the music was jazzy as opposed to melancholic. This was what Lady Merida would have wanted. Elfina and all her friends could see that. There were smiles on every face, champagne towers flowing with that golden liquid, the sweet smell of the flowers wafted in the air, and delicate desserts that touched each tongue. The people were dressed smartly in pastels and semi-formal attire, complete with whimsical hats and corsages. This party would make the late Lady feel very proud.

With all of the colorful skirts twirling like spring flowers and the giant windows opened to bring that outside-inside feel to the mansion, people opened their hearts as well as their purses. The donations that were given were enough for at least 300 miracles that went straight to the children's hospital in the Earth Realm. This is almost double what she had made for her masquerade party. Lady Merida would have been proud to be remembered in such a way and know that those in need are blessed.

*****

It's been two days since the funeral, and Elfina is standing in her store looking out the window with a fresh cup of peppermint white tea. As she feels the sunshine beaming down on her, Elfina thinks that her favorite angel must be smiling right about now. And that's why she opened her store with a breezy attitude. It's starting to get busy now, so she turns from the window and goes to her counter, watching all the patrons browse the store.

At least 20 customers are there, rushing around, trying to find what they are looking for. When Elfina sees a young fairy woman anxiously looking at every label on the aromatherapy wall, she gently approaches her.

"Are you alright, miss?" Elfina inquires, leaning her neck to the side to see the Fay's face and get her attention.

"Oh! I'm just a bundle of nerves." The fairy jumps up and down, shaking her hands. "Which one of these should I use for a first date?"

"No worries. It's something I run into all the time." Elfina assures her as she grabs a couple of seemingly random scents and points to her counter. "Follow me. I will make it up for you immediately."

Elfina goes behind the counter and grabs the bottle full of liquid oil from the South African wishing tree. She places it on the counter in front of her, kneels down, and grabs a short, empty, clear glass bottle to set it beside the oil. Elfina takes the wishing tree oil and puts it through the funnel into the glass bottle. After she finishes, she swiftly sweeps the pouring oil back into its bottle and puts it back on top of the shelf. When she heads back to the station, she makes a grab for her first scent. She remembers the list of what she has to do, which is;

Three drops of lavender to ease the fairy's anxiety, a couple of drops of rose for comfort and harmony, a drop of ylang-ylang to stimulate passion but not to an extreme level, sandalwood for balance, vanilla to release stress, and neroli to help get a second date out of the mix. Closing the glass bottle, Elfina shakes the mixture up as best as she can and voila. The concoction turns pink thanks to her natural body heat.

"There you go." Elfina smiles at her before handing the small pink glass vial to her customer. "Just put a small amount behind your ears and a drop on your wrists. You will glow to him."

"Thank you!" She giggles as she pays Elfina and skips out of the store, looking much happier than she did before.

Before she could get away from the counter, A shape-shifting customer in a business suit stopped her in her tracks. "Which ring will attract more money?"

"Actually, I just got a new shipment yesterday that will help you with that." She tells him and casually waves her arm in the invitation to her jewelry display. From inside of the glass, Elfina picks up a silver ring with three stones in it. She brings it up to the man and explains, "So, those three stones in there are tiger's eye, peridot, and pyrite. The tiger's eye will rouse hard work and determination that will pay off in the long run, peridot will attract the money coming to you, and the pyrite makes sure that prosperity is always in your corner."

A smile appears on his chestnut-brown bearded face as he puts the ring on his pinky finger. "Perfect! Thank you!"

The man pays immediately and walks away from the counter. Elfina takes the gold pieces and wanders over to her antique golden till. She pulls down the lever, and the box springs open. She puts in the money, and it disappears into the air. Elfina smiles, knowing that not only is it safe in her ether account but that it is going to bring some delicious wine to her tonight.

Suddenly, a selkie walks up to her counter. "Do you have any candles to bring out inner peace? I have a yoga class to teach in fifteen minutes. These guys are all working in the same law office, too."

"Well, let's get a candle for you then," Elfina says and leads the customer to the wall of candles. With careful consideration, Elfina picked up a tall cylinder of light blue candle that smelled like the ocean. "This is the one."

Elfina hands the candle to her, and the selkie replies, "Great!"

With that, the instructor hands Elfina the money and dashes out of the store. A few hours pass and Elfina is busy wrapping up some incense for attracting fairies to the garden for an older faun. After she handed him his purchase in a paper bag, Elfina heard someone call out.

"Excuse me, but what does this tea here do?" A young sprite calls, holding up a tea canister with a royal blue label.

"It helps you sleep." Elfina loudly replies, and the sprite nods with a pout of his round lips. With that look of a buyer's decision made, Elfina notices the leprechaun beside him, eyeing a small pan flute made of bamboo.

She smiles as she walks over to him and speaks. "You have a good eye for instruments there, sir."

"Aye." He says, looking up at her with a crooked smile. "This is a pretty little thing. Do good to call the cows with it?"

Elfina nods and explains, "Oh yes, it does that, but it also calls upon the growth of crops and grass, and if you have other animals, such as sheep or goats, it calls them too."

He continues to study the flute by turning it over and lifting the end of it to his eye. After a nod and a pout, he hands it to Elfina. "Consider it sold."

Elfina takes the flute back to her counter, wraps it up and rings up the sale. After the leprechaun leaves, Elfina continues to do her job as swarms of patrons approach her. This lasts for a few hours, and she has made so many sales today. Her heart swells with a tremendous amount of satisfaction, but at the same time, she can hardly keep her eyes open.

While she may be tired, Elfina happily turns her sign from open to closed after her last customer leaves. She takes some time to go into her office and pull out the supply list from her desk. She wants to see all that she had sold today. By the looks of this list, her jewelry went pretty fast, and the bath and body products she had just ordered went even faster. A couple of crystal clusters were sold, along with a ceramic rose and a couple of everlasting fruit trees.

Elfina stands up from her desk and goes to look at her now bare store. Luckily, she has enough stock in the back room to put out on the empty tables and shelves. Elfina's eyes light up as she studies the empty spots in her store. She has worked like crazy to make this store the wonderful place that it is today. It had surprised all the people in her circle that Elfina, the carefree nature spirit who lives in the forest and dances around spontaneously, even in her underwear, would want to own a store such as this. To make, sell, and order mystical and all-natural products for the public is not a responsibility that everyone can take on, but she does.

Spending her entire childhood with the reclusive wizard, Javas, who had taught her everything she knows about magic, has given her a purpose. It only seemed natural for her to open up her own store where she could sell her wares and knowledge.

Despite not seeing her parents for so long, they made their disapproval very apparent when she told them about it. Elfina wraps her arms around herself as she remembers that day a little over 100 years ago.

*****

"Are you crazy?!" Her father, Thor, the Norse god of lightning, bellowed at her through his long blond braided beard. "You want to open a magic store?"

40

"Not just a magic store but an experience." Elfina chimed in, trying to keep her voice even and calm. "I want to help people come into their own and feel better about themselves."

"Then be the goddess that you should have been in the first place!" Her mother, Gaia, the Greek goddess of earth, stared down at her with her anger-filled green slits for eyes. "Bad enough that you are a nymph! Now you add this onto our family?"

"I didn't ask to be a nymph! I was born that! You two made me. Why don't you take responsibility for once?!" Elfina stood up from the wooden table and slammed her palms on the table. Sick and tired of being the only composed one in this place.

But before she could say anything else, Thor interrupted her with his sky-blue eyes blazing. "Don't you take that tone with us! We are not only your parents but your betters. We can..."

"You can what?" Elfina yelled back, "Abandon me? Disown me? I was under the impression that already happened, so if you want to make good on that threat, I fully welcome it!"

With that, Elfina stormed out of the hall and towards the future that she wanted, with her parents screaming after her.

*****

Back in the present, Elfina lets out a happy sigh, knowing that she had proved her parents wrong and decides that it is time to go home. She is looking forwards to sitting outside up a tree with Iris, a cup of tea, and a piece of chocolate cake.

She wraps herself up in her shawl and steps outside her door with the key in her hand. After locking the door to her shop, Elfina walks in the direction towards Mystina Forest. As she looks up to the sky, Elfina sees a bright sunset sky that promises a clear night full of stars. To her, that means it is a perfect night for some R&R.

"Elfina!" Calls a fine, familiar voice. She turns in its direction and sees a veil-cladded Jacqueline in a sparkling ball gown with matching gloves strolling quickly towards her.

"Hi, Jacqueline!" Elfina chuckles as she approaches Jacqueline. She tries to help her lift the black heavy-set veil in order to see her face. "Honey! You are just covered. What were you doing today?"

"I was in New York City in the Earth Realm." Jacqueline laughs as she finally lifts all the veils from her face. "I had just sold some paintings down there, and I needed to pick up my fee."

"And you were worried about climate change and the polar ice caps, I take it?" Elfina jokes to her.

"Hey now! I thought Meira was the one who was going to bust our stones."

"What stones?" Elfina chuckles about the amount of taffeta that Jacqueline has adorned all over her body.

The two of them laugh as they begin to walk towards the Mystina Forest entrance. Everyone knows that vampires and sunlight don't exactly mix.

It doesn't kill them like the stories suggest, but instead, a hideous form is shown. In the darkness, vampires often look like the gorgeous, glamorous people that many tales tell of them, but when the sun hits them, it is the complete opposite. They look like demonic, dead-grey-skinned corpses that can only be found in someone's nightmares.

This is one of many reasons why vampires often are seen as evil. Luckily, the Nether Realm knows better as vampires often walk freely in the sunshine without looking like someone died. The Earth Realm, not so much. Which is why Jacqueline has her whole body covered from head to toe.

"So, you had to see Striker today?" Elfina asks, remembering Jacqueline's human familiar. "How's he doing?"

Although she has never met him, Elfina feels that she knows Striker quite well thanks to Jacqueline's renditions of him. It's like they have had many conversations together. His name is Godfrey Striker and he is considered to be an odd, somewhat sinister-looking man to a lot of people in and out of the Earth Realm.

His features are striking with his messy mop of blonde hair that sticks out in every direction and thin-squared glasses on his bulbous gray eyes. His tall, thin, lanky body is often covered in dark body-covering clothing, and his facial features almost look skeletal.

"He's doing just fine," Jacqueline answers as they walk on. "He has the asexual meet-n-greet that he is hosting in his gallery. I don't know why; he doesn't care for people being around him."

Elfina nods but has an understanding of him. "Maybe, but it is still good to know that there are people out there who are like you in an intimate fashion. If only to feel that you are not alone."

"Yes, that's true." Jacqueline agrees. "As long as I have known the man. He has never had a relationship like that of any kind. I always worried about that with him."

Jacqueline is fond of Striker but never in a romantic kind of way. Despite his eccentric looks and lifestyle, Striker is a top-notch salesman. Both Jacqueline and Elfina have a deep respect for him. Jacqueline remembers the evening that they had first met.

*****

He was sitting on a bench outside of an art gallery, looking completely dejected. Jacqueline was strolling along carrying a couple of canvases in a big black bag. She saw that sad sack there and sat beside him. She never knew why she cared but Jacqueline had a feeling that she needed to meet him.

"What's eating you tonight?" She said in a saucy, slinky voice.

Striker looked at her with a mopey expression and, instead of saying his usual, "Mind your own business, bitch!" He just looked at her and told her. "I just got fired from this bullshit gallery, who doesn't know a Rembrandt from a drainpipe."

"You told them that did you?" Jacqueline inquired with a half smile on her dark red lips.

He snorted at her and said, "No. They said it was because I made no sales. But how can I when they won't let me actually talk to the clients? I mean, I know art! I've studied art history at NYU, for Christs' sake!"

Jacqueline studied him for a moment and pulled out the canvases from her bag. "Do you think you can sell these right now?"

Striker's expression became both suspicious and curious until he looked from her to the paintings. As soon as he gazed at them, he was mesmerized. "These are exquisite. The shadow compositions and the one streak of dark blue. I haven't seen anything like this!"

Jacqueline let out an amused grin, looked at her paintings, and pointed down at each one as she explained, "Yes, this is what I call my "Children of the Night Series." I get a lot of inspiration from the darkness."

Striker could see why she did. The paintings were in black and white with a few streaks of royal blue to offset the mood. One had stars over a night sky with a flock of bats flying towards a full moon, another was of a rat outside of a sewer grate, and the last was a white albeit shadowed hand reaching up from the ground.

"I could sell these easily." He said with a burst of confidence.

"Really? Show me then." Jacqueline challenged the befuddled man. He looked at her and smiled wickedly like a silent promise.

True to his word, he did just that. Despite his eccentric looks, Jacqueline could tell that Striker knew his stuff when it came to sales. He had sold her paintings in 30 minutes. The way he spoke about them had art lovers desperately buying what he was willing to sell and in cash no less. Suffice it to say, Jacqueline was impressed.

Striker walked back to her with a large sum of cash in his hand. "There you are, sold all three for $5,000."

"Excellent!" Jacqueline stood up and held her hand out, not for the money but to shake his hand. As they shook hands, she piped up. "You have earned twice as much as this gallery would have sold these paintings for. Have you ever thought of owning a gallery of your own?"

"Well, I…"

"Because I have a proposition for you," Jacqueline suggested. "Some people and I have a warehouse with a loft living space in it. We are looking for someone to run it as a gallery of our own. What say you?"

Not needing to think about it, Striker only shook his head yes, enthusiastically. Since that day, Striker became familiar willingly. It took time for him to realize that she was a vampire nevertheless, that surprisingly didn't phase him. But Jacqueline had never told Elfina that story yet.

*****

"Maybe that's why he's holding an asexual meeting," Elfina says, snapping Jacqueline out of her memory. "To meet someone as like-minded as he is."

Jacqueline just shrugs, "Maybe."

"So, how popular is your art over there in the Earth Realm?" Elfina probes with an interested look on her face.

"Darling! My paintings are a hit." She answers with a proud, wide grin that slightly shows her hidden fangs. "Thank you to the goths, art lovers, and teenagers going through dark phases."

With a laugh from both of them, they walk on to the entrance of the forest, enjoying each other's company. Just before the two of them reach the forest, Jacqueline taps Elfina's shoulder.

"Oh! Don't forget that the vampires are hosting a gala tomorrow night to which you are cordially invited."

Elfina stops, smiles, and faces her friend at the entrance of the forest. "Don't worry, I haven't forgotten and I got a new dress for the occasion. It starts just before dusk, right?"

"Yes." Jacqueline nods and points a glove-clad finger at her. "As you know, it is an elegant affair, so I hope your new dress impresses and Daniel will be there too."

As Jacqueline arches her eyebrow, Elfina shakes her head in amusement. Of course, Jacqueline is still trying to set her up with Daniel. He is a vampire that is a little younger than she is but he already has her seal of approval. His suave sophisticated manner and charming personality could win over even the most frigid of mystics. Especially since he always looks so good in a suit. Elfina does think he is handsome and when they first met, she had a little crush on him. Sadly, they both know that they could only ever really be good friends. He is always good company and has interesting stories to tell. That is why she is always happy to hear that he will be at a party.

"Great! Tomorrow night then." Elfina gives Jacqueline a hug goodbye.

"Yes. The carriage will pick you up after you close your shop." Jacqueline declares releasing her friend from the embrace.

"Awesome!" Elfina affirms enthusiastically and begins to walk inside the forest. She looks back and gives a wave to Jacqueline. "I'll see you soon."

"Will do!" Jacqueline answers returning the wave and turning towards the road. "Take care, Darling."

As Jacqueline walks towards the road where her black gothic carriage awaits her, Elfina turns towards the forest path. She gazes up at the trees and allows herself to be swept away in its glorious ambiance. The smell of it alone is a mixture of cherry blossoms, lemongrass, and pine needles. A strange combination to be true, but somehow, it just works.

The trees themselves have a rainbow of colors surrounding them, as if magic itself is protecting the forest from all negativity. When a being is on the ground, you can see all the colors in a way that looks like it is some kind of light show. However, if they were flying above in the sky with a set of wings or the help of a winged animal, they would see something a little different. From the sky, the trees have one solid color where. Each looks like a vibrant picture that has been altered in a most impressive way.

As Elfina walks through this vibrant forest, she feels a gentle breeze brush through her hair as if it is saying, "Welcome home."

That is what this forest is to her: home. To see these bright green plants under the trees and the tiny multicoloured wildflowers nestling under those fills her with gratitude. It is a wonderful place to live in this forest the way she does. Although she is a very sociable woman, Elfina loves that not too many creatures live in this forest. She can have that peace and quiet that she needs every so often, thanks to that fact. This is her haven.

Sadly, this is short-lived thanks to an uninvited guest popping out of one of the bushes beside her.

"Did I hear something about a party?" The disgusting smarmy sod with a lecherously large grin on his round little face announces.

Elfina sighs as she struggles to keep her annoyance with the small faun-like god under control. "Would it matter if I said no, Pan?"

Something like a smirk escapes from his thin lips, "Certainly not, but I know you're going to need some of my special wine, my beautiful beloved."

Elfina continues on her journey home and tries to ignore the short little nuisance following her on his spry goat legs. He skips in front of her and shows her the same red wine that he keeps trying to impress her with. "Such as this wine, perhaps?"

"Pan, as I said last week and for pretty much my entire womanhood, I will never drink that drug-laden wine that you keep trying to foist on me and pretty much everything else with a vagina." She says sternly while passing him by.

Still too dumb not to take a hint, Pan continues to trot beside her. "Well, my dear, a stunning nymph such as yourself should not be without even the smallest of pleasures, such as a fine wine. After all, this fine wine is made by my finest," He pauses as he trails his maple-colored eyes up and down her slender, lithe body, "grapes, of course."

"I, nor any nymph for that matter, are interested in you," She pauses in the same way he did, only for this purpose to mock him. She moves her eyes to his cloth-covered crotch and backs up to his eyes. "Grapes Pan."

She pushes herself forwards, but he does not leave her side or stop bothering her. "You don't invite me to your house anymore, my dear."

Elfina stops in her tracks and faces him once again. "Now that is just ridiculous, Pan. I never once invited you to my house in the first place."

Before she could turn back and head towards the direction of her house, Pan blinked his eyes to teleport himself in front of her to block her path.

"I can't begin to think of why that is either." He articulates archly as he leans up against the tree closest to him.

"It's really quite simple, Pan." She pronounces, matching his mischievous tone with a coyly flippant tone of her own. Elfina leans forward, grabs his dark brown goateed chin, and curtly tells. "I don't like you."

Any man would have taken the hint and backed off, but of course, not Pan. She steps over his leaning body and walks on home without looking back. A challenged smile appears on his face as he watches her walk away with lustful fascination.

"I love a feisty nymph." He sniffs at the air and disappears into the air.

Elfina stops in front of her door and shakes her head. She knows that this isn't over. Pan will be back and be just as bothersome. Luckily, he never crossed any boundaries because if he did, that would be a punishment that he could never spend his eternal life with.

Elfina smiles wickedly as she puts her key into her door and remembers what that punishment would be if he were to even rape a woman like he has been known to do in the past. His penis would slowly shrivel up and die off.

"Would serve him right," Elfina whispers to herself as she steps inside her house.

Chapter Four

The moon tower stands tall and proud in the moonlit night. A little more so than usual tonight it seems. The harmonious melodies of classical music flow through its dark, gleaming walls. The tower itself looks like a grand black grotto that reaches for the starry sky like an exotic flower just waiting to bloom. This structure is surrounded by a dark forest that has no name. Elfina is taking the vampire's carriage through it right now.

The forest itself is deemed creepy by most of the folks in the Nether Realm. She could see why with the twisted, dead-looking trees, the soggy foggy ground that lays below, and the fact that both vampires and werewolves have been known to hunt in there from time to time. It is also typical to see some ghosts roaming around on a seemingly aimless path. To her, Elfina did not find this place as bad as most did. The trees, although macabre are not dead. The ghosts are harmless and don't bother anyone. Lastly, when any kind of hunt is on, be it vampires or werewolves, the forest is always closed off to keep any civilians from being harmed. Elfina thinks that this forest is nothing more than an interesting piece of scenery to watch before you come to and from the Moon Tower.

When Elfina arrives, she steps out of the carriage, trying to be as graceful as she can be by lightly touching her foot to the ground. Tonight, she wore satin pumps to the event and is just hoping that she did not sink into the ground. Luckily, the gravel ground is hard, and she does not. She looks down and has one last check of her outfit to make sure that it is appropriate for this event. Her gown is a backless royal blue velvet gown with a wide skirt. She has set it off with white pearls dangling from her neck to her navel. Her long blonde hair is swept back with matching pearl combs. With this ensemble, she did not know how she could not be perfectly dressed for this occasion. Elfina spun around and looked up towards the white translucent man who was driving the carriage.

"Thank you, Henry." She says with a happy sparkle in her eye and passes him a single gold coin.

"You are most welcome, Elfina." He says, sharing a beaming smile towards her before suddenly remembering what his wife wanted him to ask her. "Say Elfina, do you have anymore holy cups in your store? The wife and I would love to be alive when we head out for our vacation in Atlantis next week."

"I will have a shipment of them tomorrow," Elfina speaks to the spectre. "You will love Atlantis. It's the most beautiful paradise ever!"

Elfina flashes her hands for effect, and Henry chuckles. "Yes. My wife showed me those pictures of yours. Now she has to go."

"Well, you two deserve a nice vacation, Henry. How long has it been?"

"Too long." Henry happily nods to her and gives a salute. "I'll see you tomorrow then?"

Elfina gives him a bigger smile and waves her hand to him. "Drive safely, Henry."

After Henry gives a cluck of his dead tongue, the red-eyed horse moves forwards with the carriage. Elfina turns towards the heavy-set vampire that is guarding the door to the tower. Although he is built like a stone golem, the man is dressed smartly in a pin-stripe suit and bowler hat. Elfina ran through her small pouch to find the invitation that Jacqueline had given her. He continues to stare at her suspiciously. Elfina gets the feeling he is trying to be intimidating, but it didn't phase her. She pulls out the invitation as it unfolds itself and does not reveal a single crease.

A black-colored invitation written in silver calligraphy reads, "Vampire Moonlight Gala: You are invited!"

Elfina beams at the guard and hands him the invitation. With a sniff and a huff, he stands off to the side. "Enter here and have a good night, Miss."

"You too," Elfina says, matching his stoic, somewhat grumpy demeanor with her natural bubbly cheer.

Upon entering the tower, Elfina looks around the dark hallway. Dark brass candelabras were placed on each side of the stairway, going up six steps at a time to light the way. Elfina follows the blood-red carpet that decorates the floor at her feet. It is the only source of color here, as the clear glass windows in an intricate spiderweb pattern show off the delicate moonlight. Portraits of the vampire coven members adorn the wall beside her. It gave almost a dramatic, if not watchful, presence to the place. Elfina recognizes the work of each painting. All of them were done by Jacqueline. That woman's talent never ceases to amaze.

After walking up many flights of this spiraling staircase, Elfina finally reaches the top of the tower. The grand ballroom is here, just before the gigantic designed curvy-lined door that looks like it belongs in a royal cemetery as opposed to an event room.

The doors slowly fly open, and Elfina sees how the grand room is filled with people. The smells of wine and perfume waft through the air, along with the sounds of laughter and chatter. She looks around the room and can feel the beautiful gothic romance that only the vampires can provide.

Long white tapered candles sit in several different black-colored candelabras of all sizes that are strewn out throughout the room. Burgundy-colored chaises circle around a blood-red Persian rug. A long, black intricate fireplace sits at the far end of the room, with a wooden fire burning and bringing a strong ambiance into an already fierce atmosphere. A large mirror hangs over the mantle that shows off every guest in the room.

Elfina lets out a little chuckle, remembering the legend of how vampires cast no reflections in such things as mirrors, lakes, or other reflective surfaces. Oh, how wrong that legend is. She knows that all she has to do is look into any mirror and there would be the vampire. It is just too silly not to laugh about it.

"Elfina!" Jacqueline gracefully waves and walks over to Elfina. She kisses both of her cheeks as soon as she approaches. "Somehow, I knew you would be coming."

Elfina matches Jacqueline's arched eyebrow with a wicked expression of her own. "What can I say? A good friend invited me and who would never forgive me if I didn't show up. Besides, I would never miss a good party."

Elfina gives her friend a wink. With a laugh on both sides, Jacqueline links her arm with Elfina's and the two of them begin to circle the party. Jacqueline looks as regal as ever in her black shoulder-baring taffeta gown with short sleeves. Her long, pale arms did not have a sign of chilliness despite how cold they felt on Elfina's arm. Her nails were also painted a bright red that matched the blood that was drizzling down the champagne tower in the center of the room.

The two of them reached the bar, and there stood an impeccably dressed bartender in a black and white tuxedo. He is wiping down the wine glass in his hand with a clean black towel. Without even talking to him, Jacqueline picks up a martini glass filled with blood, within reach of her.

Elfina looks happily from Jacqueline to the bartender and sweetly rests her head on her hands, "Hi, Jeremy. You have got a busy night tonight."

"Welcome back, Elfina." He says tipping his bowler hat to her and giving her a friendly fanged smile. "What can I get you tonight?"

"I'll take whichever sweet red wine that you have tonight."

With a nod to her, he bangs on the bar, which makes a wine bottle flip in the air. The show of his bartending skills. He catches the bottle by its nose spins around on his heel while tossing it behind his back. After he catches it, he quickly pours her requested wine into a wide-rimmed wine glass and hands it to her. Jacqueline and Elfina link their arms together again and turn towards the party again. The two of them each take a sip of their respective drinks with giggles to spare.

Suddenly, standing before them a few feet away is a slick blonde-haired man with youthful good looks and a sharp-looking suit. This is the vampire, Daniel, whom Jacqueline has been trying to fix Elfina up with for years.

Jacqueline points one of her long, slender fingers to him. "You should go talk to him, dear. He likes you. He's a gentleman and one that is quite pleasing to the eye if you ask me." Elfina looks at her friend with a combination of suspicion and amusement. "Go be the little flirt we all know you to be."

Elfina scoffs at her and smiles. "I guess you have me there. Chat with you later?"

"Of course. I want details."

Elfina shakes her head and walks over to Daniel, leaving her friend to watch everything unfold. Stephan walks over to his wife with a beer in his hand. He is truly handsome in his tuxedo, which Jacqueline insists he wears to these parties. His sand-colored hair is short and spikey, with a stubble of a beard just beginning on his golden-tanned face. His eyes are the same color as a beautiful clear blue sky on a bright sunny day. At this moment, he looks both rugged and romantic. He takes his free arm and wraps it around his wife's tiny waist.

"So, I see you're still trying to fix up your friend to be married, eh?" He says amusedly, pulling her close to him and pressing his lips gently to her neck. Jacqueline closes her eyes and lets the ecstasy of her mate's touch wash over her. She gives a low, pleasing purr before she lets out a lusty leer and turns to look up at Stephan.

"I just want her to be happy." She utters as she takes a quick glance over to Elfina before she looks into her husband's eyes and embraces him. "Like I am with you.

He leans down and gives Jacqueline a slow but mindful caress on the mouth with his nicely thin lips. When he pulls away, Stephan studies his wife. "Have I told you how beautiful you look tonight?"

He leans down and trails some sweet, tiny kisses along her jaw.

"Yes, but I don't mind hearing it again." She pulls him closer to feel his body warm up against hers. "I have a feeling you are trying to distract me because you want to leave the party a little early tonight?"

Stephan looks down at her lovingly and feels the heat fill his loins like a rapidly spreading forest fire. "You know that I love our parties better."

Jacqueline snickers up at him. "I do, too but we do have to be a little more social." She pauses to take one last look at Elfina, chatting it up with Daniel. "After all. My best friend has just arrived, and I want her to have a good time too."

She links her fingers with her husband's and takes a step back. The two of them walk to the sofa hand in hand.

As Elfina approaches Daniel, he takes her hand and lightly presses his lips to her knuckles as he wishes to greet her like a proper gentleman. "Elfina. You are as beautiful as ever."

"Thank you, Daniel. You are looking very dapper yourself tonight." She sways her body ever so subtly.

Elfina is looking forward to having a good conversation with Daniel. No one makes flirting as fun as he does. This is a male vamp who has many good stories and riveting intelligence with his easy smile and carefree charm. Elfina finds herself relaxing with ease.

"How is your shop doing?" He asks, swirling his wine glass.

"Well, with vacation season coming up in a couple of days, it'll be busy pretty quick," Elfina says taking a sip of her wine. "How about you? How's the vineyard?"

Holding his arm out to Elfina, she slips her arm around it, and they walk together around the party. "Well, I have just created this sexy merlot that I have in my glass right now. I think it is going to take the Earth Realm by storm and hopefully this dimension too."

Elfina looks up at him and lifts an eyebrow. "Are you trying to get me to try that wine, Daniel?"

With a mischievous sneer, he says. "Did it work?"

"Yes." Elfina laughs. "If you bring me one, I will meet you on the sofa with Jacqueline and Stephan."

"Done." He affirms as they click their wine glasses collectively.

As Daniel turns to head back to the bar, Elfina floats herself through the crowd towards the sofa where Jacqueline and Stephan are sitting. Nods of recognition and quick hellos were given by both her and the other party patrons, but eventually, Elfina made it to that long burgundy sofa in a matter of seconds. There, Jacqueline nestles close to a smiling Stephan with his arm wrapped around her bare shoulders. Elfina feels her heart warm at the cute couple that is sitting before her. With a sigh, she sits next to Jacqueline.

Lifting her glass to the two of them, Elfina chimes in, "I hope I didn't interrupt the love-in, you guys."

"Of course not, darling," Jacqueline reassures her friend as she lifts her glass to her. "We were just enjoying watching the action for a change."

Elfina nods and looks over to Stephan, who is sipping his beer. She could tell that he was just waiting for this party to end. He wants to spend some "quality" time with his wife, and Elfina could not blame him for that. By the look of his lusty eyes tracing Jacqueline's body, it didn't take a psychiatrist to see those wheels in his brain turning.

Elfina, who is always the hopeless romantic, can't help but swoon at the sight of seeing two people so in love. She often plays a game with herself where she creates secret stories for any couple that crosses her path. Like Gabriel with his mate, the moon spirit Luna. Right now, he is standing over by the fireplace sipping his wine glass full of blood while she is standing and chatting with Valerie and Willa. Like clockwork, the two of them look at each other at the exact same time as if they called

56

out to each other with their minds with that loving look and knowing smile, It is easy to see that even after 1000 years of being together, they can almost talk to each other without even opening their mouths.

Then there is Valerie and her lover Willa, who are talking to Luna. They are holding hands at the moment but in a quick second they turn to look at each other. In a combination of love and habit, they press their lips together and break apart to go in different directions. Willa walks towards the restroom and Valerie goes back to talking to Luna. Whenever they had to separate, they always gave each other a quick peck goodbye. The two of them have such a subtle but sublime intimacy that would make anyone a little envious.

Elfina loves the Nether Realm for this reason. It does not matter who you love but that you are loved. She looks back over to Jacqueline and Stephan. These two are the product of true love. The sweet intimate glances, the tender glances and the way they twine their fingers together when they sit together. It's completely unmistakable that they have a good if not great marriage. Sure, they have problems just like anyone else but Elfina knows that the two of them always pull together despite how different they are on the surface.

One such example of this is that every now and again, Jacqueline will go hunting with Stephan and his pack.

*****

The first time they went on a hunt was nearly 300 years ago. It was not exactly a smooth first run. It was the night after their wedding when a bright blue full moon seemed bigger than even the whole of the world.

Stephan was facing his pack of five other wolves. This included the pack alpha (who is now retired) named Demetri who was an older-looking man with grey hairs stemming from his black facial hair. Next to him was Anna, his mate and second-in-command who was a shapely woman with a fierce look in her amber eyes. Followed by Piet who is a tall albeit friendly man who was ready with a smile on his face. Jess, the fiery and impetuous pup who is the youngest of the pack, stands next to Stephan. And lastly was Mara, the quiet and shy wolf who was not afraid to pounce on any prey that came her way. The whole group looked at Stephan and saw that he brought his new wife with him.

They did not bother hiding their distain for having her there. The five of them growled and snarled at her. Jacqueline did not even quiver, but she did return their snarls with one of her own. Stephan held her hand and gave it a comforting squeeze, nonetheless to both calm and comfort.

"My wife hunts with us!" Stephan bellowed at the angry pack members. "She is a part of this pack now as I am a part of her coven!"

"That is not what we are angry about," Anna said with a hushed but deadly tone. "Why is she dressed in that get-up?"

Jacqueline looked down at her black robe volante with white trim at the bodice. She had just gotten it from Paris and had wanted to show it off. With a look of disappointment written on her face and the anger of her new husband's pack, it did not get the reception that she had hoped it would.

"Stephan." Demetri tried to sound patient but the annoyance in his voice came out instead. "We had just approved of the Vampire-Werewolf Matrimony Clause but if she is to hunt with us, she must be set up and ready to hunt as any of us would be."

"Vampires hunt a little different than us lycanthropes." Stephan chimed in. "You all know that. She should be able to hunt just the way she chooses to."

"If she is one of us, then…" Stephan put his hand up to Demetri, silencing him.

"By marriage she is!" He began and slowly lowered his hand down to continue what he was saying. "She will hunt as she deems necessary just as we will. There will be no more issue for that." Stephan paused for a moment and looked at Demetri. "Anyone who wishes to

58

challenge me on that will do so in battle, even if that means I become the new alpha."

The rest of the wolves looked to Demetri. They all thought that he would be the one to say something, but instead, his face morphed into a look of pride. He gave Stephan a little half-smile and let out a roar of laughter. Looks of wide-eye surprise crossed everyone else's faces as Demetri continued to bellow out his hardy laugh.

"Very good, Stephan." He said breathlessly pointing his finger at him.

Stephan scrunched his face at Demetri. "What?"

"You are a good wolf indeed." He said calming down a little more. "You truly have become a fine man."

All the wolves gathered around Demetri while Stephan stayed where he was, still holding Jacqueline's hand. She took his hand in both of hers, silently promising that she would not leave him. That she was there and was going to stay. Demetri walked up to the both of them with an enigmatic expression on his heavily bearded face.

"A wolf must always stand by his mate even against the challenges of others. Only then can he call himself a true wolf." Demetri said and patted Stephan's shoulder like he was a proud father. "You will make a fine alpha one day."

There was no higher praise than that, especially since it came from a pack leader. Stephan and Jacqueline stood there dumbfounded by what had just happened. Quite frankly, so was the rest of the pack. That was when Demetri turned and faced the rest of the pack.

"Well, what are we waiting for?" He shouted with joy and waved his hands up in the air. "Let us hunt!"

After his words, the members of Stephan's pack morphed into their wolf forms. In a matter of minutes, the wolves darted into the forest. Stephan turned to Jacqueline and took her in his arms. He held her close; he breathed in the scent of her hair and placed his forehead on top of hers.

"My love." He whispered to her. "No one tells me or my wife how she must hunt."

Jacqueline looked up at him with affectionate eyes. She knew what he really meant by that statement. He was telling her that no one would ever tell him who to love. The two of them realized that this was their first test and obstacle as a married couple. By the loving look that they shared at that moment, they had passed this obstacle and are ready to face whatever may come next.

*****

The two of them are looking at each other this way right now. Elfina gave them a starry-eyed smile, thinking how cool it is that Jacqueline, the classy take-no-crap vampire and Stephan, the easy-going every-wolfman, could be the best couple that Elfina has ever known.

She looks around at all the people in the room and notices that someone is missing. "Hey? Where is Nico?"

Jacqueline peeks around with Elfina and notices his absence as well. "I'm not sure. I haven't seen him for a while." With a casual shrug of her shoulders, Jacqueline continues her statement. "I imagine that he's out walking around somewhere. Besides he is usually gone for a couple of days at a time."

"But he never misses a party, Babe." Stephan stares with the same concern that Elfina has. "That's not like him at all."

"True, but even he needs a break every now and then. I'm sure it's nothing to be concerned about, you two." Jacqueline calmly explains. "I guarantee to you both that we will see him tomorrow."

Both Elfina and Stephan look at each other and nod in agreement. It is more than likely that Jacqueline is right as Nico does tend to disappear when he wants to. Soon Daniel approaches Elfina, holding a glass of red wine in a round wine glass.

"Here you are my dear," Daniel says leaning over dramatically at Elfina and handing her the glass of wine. "This sexy little vino will kick any Greek wine's ass back to Mount Olympus."

Seeing the wayward, defiant expression on his face, Elfina lifts her eyebrow and accepts his challenge with a defying look of her own. She takes the glass of wine and has a sip while keeping her eyes on Daniel's smug face. It is a sexy little number. It has a sharp, robust taste with little woody notes that she could not resist. Like all nymphs, Elfina has a special love for wine, not just for its taste and structure but for how it makes a person feel.

"Very nice Daniel," Elfina sips the wine flirtatiously. "You do have a wonderful gift for wine."

"Ever since I was a human, my dear." He says as he sits next to her on the sofa and puts his arm around the back of it in an almost affectionate way without crossing any boundaries. His eyes grow dreamy as he gazes up to the ceiling and recalls. "I was a small boy growing up in Venice, Italy. The waterways and architecture are still wonderful there. And then there is the beach, which is just as delightful. I still love that old family's farm. The small house is no longer there but it still holds everything so precious. Beautiful."

As he trails off, Elfina pipes up with a smile. "It sounds fabulous."

"It is." Daniel smiles a little wider and turns to behold Elfina. "You could come and see for yourself if you ever wanted to. I would love to have you."

He picks up her hand and kisses it lightly again. "I appreciate that, Daniel, but I don't really go to the Earth Realm that much. I'm too busy here."

She knows that she isn't completely telling him the whole truth at that time. She turns away from him, feeling a little guilty about it. The truth is that she never goes to the Earth Realm because it scares her to death. Human nature shocks her. Throughout her whole long life,

Elfina has heard stories about how many nymphs before her were broken-hearted, mistreated, or even raped in that realm by humans. She did not want that to happen to her. She takes a glimpse at the ceiling and remembers every excuse she has ever given.

"I can't get away from the store. I have a date tonight. Or I am vacationing somewhere else this time." She can hear herself saying these to anyone who asks. Then she thinks to herself, "Why would I go to that dimension when this one suits me so well?"

She looks back over at Daniel, gives him a friendly smile and leans up against his shoulder like she has done so many times. She is so happy here in the Nether Realm right now, and she will not have it tarnished with any bad memories from another world. Not letting anything darken her evening, Elfina brings her focus back to the present and enjoys the party. With a red wine in her hand and a few good friends sitting with her on the sofa, she realizes that tonight is a good night. She will not let any negative feelings spoil that for her.

Chapter Five

Elfina loves having a day off. After the vampire party and a few good days at the store, where she sold out nearly all of her stock, she feels that she deserves a day where she can have some fun and do whatever she wants. To her mind, the best thing about having her own business is that she can take one day off or several if she desires to do so. This is the kind of freedom that Elfina lives for.

Today, she is sitting outside on a street patio in a little café in the town of knowledge known as Scalars. In this quaint little city, there is one of the best universities in the Nether Realm. As she sips her hibiscus peach green tea, Elfina's eyes trail themselves to that university. The multi-colored bulb-like towers reach the sky like flowers reaching for the sun. In that school, the possibilities are endless, and it is believed that as soon as you walk through its doors, your destiny unfolds. They study everything like magic, martial arts, science, business, astrology, and so much more.

Elfina finds this to be true as she is living proof of this. She stretches out her long legs and slips off her brown sandals. She tugs on the sleeve of her flowing green tunic and brushes her hands against her brown pants in an old habit. She does this every time she begins to remember something, and right now, she is remembering her and Viola's time there.

*****

A younger version of Viola and Elfina stood on the wide steps just before that big bulbous bright building. Elfina's hair was the same length it always was but Viola's jet-black hair was long and straight as a younger woman has. They said nothing; just looked up at this school in silent awe. Both of them were dressed in their school uniforms of a burgundy blazer with the Scalars crest imprinted on the breast pocket, crisp white blouses, and plaid skirts that matched the blazers. Feeling both nervous and excited at the same time the two of them took each other's hands and gave a comforting squeeze as a way to give each other strength.

"Imagine, it's our first day here." Viola said as she let go of Elfina's hand and pushed her long black hair behind her ear. "This will shape our lives into something meaningful just by being here."

As Viola adjusted her backpack, Elfina raised her eyebrow and smiled at her friend, "I'm pretty sure we already did that when we decided what we wanted to do with our lives."

"True but it can come true much faster now." Viola spoke giddily to her friend as she snapped her fingers. At this time, Viola didn't tell Elfina that she did not know what she wanted to do as far as her career was concerned. But if she was to find her destiny, it would be in this place. After all, the legends of the Nether Realm do say that your destiny is guaranteed to be found at Scalars University. Viola was determined to find hers.

"Well at least we can agree on that." Elfina put her arm around her friend's shoulders and gave her a quick hug. She looked in the direction of where her first class was and began to walk towards it. "Well, my dear, I have to go to my entrepreneurial class. See you at lunch?"

"Yeah, see you then!" Viola called out to her with a wave.

Elfina walked on to her class while Viola stayed at the stoop just to indulge in one more breath of fresh air. After taking in that sweet air, Viola straightened out her skirt and walked up the stairs to go to her first class.

It did not take long for the lunch break to roll around. Elfina and Viola sat together outside at this little café that has the perfect view of the school. The sweet little bistro tables and cobblestone streets made it the perfect place to talk about their latest and most welcome adventure of their first classes.

"I've met some really nice-looking guys in my class." Elfina piped up as she took her first sip of tea. "I think it'll be really fun getting to know them."

"Is that all you have learned from your classes today, Elfina?" Viola asked, matching her friend's playful look with her own.

"No! I also learned some good fundamentals for my store." Elfina answered. "Did you know that marshmallow is not only good for your health but it repairs bone?" When Viola shook her head, Elfina smiled and noticed how she was fidgeting in her chair. Elfina could not help but let out an amused chuckle at seeing her friend's eagerness. She was just waiting for her to ask. "So, how were your classes then?"

"Good! I like my banking professor." Viola said, looking somewhat dreamily at the table where her uneaten shrimps were sitting. "I think I might have a knack for banking."

"Oh?" Elfina inquired, lifting both of her eyebrows. She knew her friend too well to know that the starry-eyed look meant a lot more than just a simple liking to someone. "Banking? I thought just taking that class would piss your parents off."

"No, of course not! That is not it. They do expect great things from me, though." Viola corrected her friend in the proper manner that she does when she gets annoyed. However, being the sharp siren that she is, she does intend to turn the tables. "Besides, aren't your parents angry with the fact that you are here to learn how to run your own store?"

"Who cares?" Elfina casually waved her hand and took another sip of her tea. "Everything pisses them off. Now tell me about this banking class."

"Well, I seemed to ace the basics of money already." Viola chimed in after she ate a shrimp off of her plate. "Armand said so himself."

"Armand?" Elfina said coquettishly as she picked up a carrot stick. "Your teacher, I take it."

"Yes."

Elfina raised an eyebrow at her and snapped at the carrot stick with her teeth. "It's not the banking you are interested in, is it?"

"Yes, it is." Viola looked up at Elfina with her eyes wide in shock. She spoke up in a defensive tone but soon she did admit. "But there is something appealing about Armand."

Elfina nodded and smiled at her friend. Viola was always easy to read, even when she tried not to be. Elfina could clearly see that dear sweet Viola has a classic case of "passion a le professor." It was nice to see that. Elfina had hoped that this would get her normally shy friend out of her shell a little more. Viola had stayed there much longer than Elfina did but that was no surprise. Elfina only wanted to take some entrepreneurial classes, while Viola chose to study the business world as a whole. This is why she is one of the best underwater bankers of her time.

*****

Back in the present, Elfina knows that it did not really happen like that for poor Viola and decides to put that part of the past out of her mind. This is not the time to go reminiscing about fallen hopes and broken hearts, especially when it happened to one of her best friends. So, she continues to eat her lunch of the vegetarian power bowl of tofu, sweet potatoes, and broccoli with an Asian sesame sauce that she ordered. It does seem like a day for spicy things especially when the martial arts students are practicing across from her at the town square. A wicked smile spreads on her face as she contemplates the fact that she is having dinner and a show.

Suddenly, her view is interrupted by a group of Valkyries patrolling by. Elfina is prepared to ignore them as she tries to lean away from the obstruction of her view. However, she hears the words "the vampire, Nico," come out of the blonde-haired Valkyrie's mouth. Elfina discreetly tunes into their conversation.

"They keep claiming that these are just rumors but we are going to have to tell people about this eventually." The red-headed woman says as she takes off her golden-winged helmet and brushes a hand through her hair. "Everyone seems to be in danger, and these demons are attacking at random."

"What good would telling everybody do?" The raven-haired African-descended one asks. "All we would do is cause a mass panic, giving the demon or demons exactly what they want."

"Something has to be done though."

"Yes, and we better do it before it strikes a fourth person."

Fourth? Elfina thinks to herself. *Is there a third person who got hurt?*

As the three Valkyries walk off, Elfina finds her stomach twisted up in knots, and her heart increases with worry. Clearly, what is happening with these demons now is no longer just rumors but a frightening reality. Too many people are getting killed, and it is time to look into this situation.

Although she had planned to see him anyway, Elfina decides that after her stop at the market, she will see Javas right away. If anyone can shed some light on what is happening with these demons, it's her old guardian. Besides, he is the one person she could always go to if there is ever any trouble. He always took better care of her than her own parents ever did. That's why she always thought of him more as a father figure as well as a teacher. His specialty is magic, holistics, and fortune-telling. So, it makes sense that he might know something about this.

With a sigh escaping her lips, Elfina finishes her tea, stands up, and straightens out her pants. She has to stop at the market to pick up Javas' groceries as well as her own. She walks over to the giant greenhouse-like building which is the food market that she always enjoys going to. It is expensive but sometimes a person deserves a treat. Grocery shopping for Elfina is a lot like meditation.

She walks in, and the smell of fresh fruit and vegetables brings a wonderfully earthy sensation to her lungs. The bright sparkle of the clear windows shines in the sun, while the clean blue sky reflects through the glass, making all the beauteous fresh food inside look that much more colorful.

She begins to walk along the produce aisle, admiring all the fruits and vegetables that are on sale. Feeling safe and warm once again, Elfina's carefree, optimistic manner returns.

"Elfina!" Calls a friendly voice from a stout, bearded man as he tosses a red apple in her direction.

She graciously accepts the fruit with a smile and puts it into her rainbow purse. "Thanks, Jean!"

Elfina walks over to the aisle of chocolate, deciding that she needs more of her favorite vice. She stops and looks down the aisle, and her eyes light up at such a wonderful sight. Several different shapes, sizes, and flavors of chocolate are lined up, just waiting for her to grab them, but only one thing grabs her attention. At the end of the aisle itself is a large chocolate fondue fountain with its daily special being highlighted. Elfina walks over to it and looks at the floating chalkboard sign with the flavor of chocolate written in pink cursive writing.

"Pink Peppercorn Dark Chocolate." It reads.

Elfina smiles at that as she takes a bamboo skewer and sticks a strawberry through it. Without any hesitation, she sticks the strawberry in the pouring chocolate, removes it, and takes a greedy bite of the slowly hardening dessert. The pep of the pepper hits her first, and then suddenly, the richness of the chocolate takes over.

"That's it!" She announces to herself and to a couple of mystics around her. She looks cheerfully at the others and says, "I will take this chocolate."

She kneels down and grabs a good-sized bar of chocolate that sits underneath the fountain's display. The two other mystics smile and nod at her. Elfina can't read minds but she has the sneaking suspicion that they think she is crazy. Not that she cares or anything. With a spring in her step, she continues her grocery-shopping adventure.

Elfina observes how the employees over the counters are trying to get the customers to buy an item that might bring both nourishment and joy into their lives. When Elfina came here for her university classes, she found that just by watching how others bought and sold their wares. She had gotten some good knowledge on how to sell her own merchandise.

As Elfina stands and watches the fire dragon chili demonstration, she remembers how she would drag Viola here just to people-watch. Viola would just analyze everything that was going on, but to Elfina it was fun. Besides, Viola didn't know it but she got to see how the monetary system worked in business. This helped her in her banking career as well.

By putting all she had learned from these merchants here and by getting to know the people in Merkiva, Elfina found her own style when it came to retail. She prospered just by being herself. A grateful smile blooms on her face as she snaps out of her daydream and turns towards the checkout tills.

A tall, dark figure bumps into her, which causes her head to turn to the right slightly and gently grab onto their arm for support. Suddenly, she has a vision, and her eyes snap shut. She sees what she assumes is this tall man that she bumped into. Elfina stands in the middle of a deserted cobblestone street at night. She looks towards the university and can tell that she is still in Scalars, but it is at night. The tall cottage-style buildings seem so grey and colourless that send chills up Elfina's back.

Out of the center of the stones, a black, weightless-looking mist oozes out from the ground. It is so sinister and slimy that Elfina feels her stomach sink. To her right, Elfina hears a cheerful tune being whistled. She looks in that direction and sees a blonde half-naked fairy adorned in yellow walking through the street, completely unaware of what is happening there.

Elfina turns and looks back to the mist that has only grown in size and the faerie who is stumbling towards it. She is completely intoxicated by something. Elfina lets out a gasp as she helplessly watches this faerie stumble onto her doom.

"I'll be singing all day!" The faerie sings out loud as she spins to the center of that cobblestone.

The shadow quickly turns into a humanoid figure and grabs onto the faerie girl's arm. She lets out a series of giggles and looks up at him.

"Sorry! Tonight's so great! You're so great!" She laughs out loud as she puts her hand on his arm.

The faerie's face falls when she realizes what is happening. The shadow creature's pale face contorts as his lips twist into a hollow crack. A black ooze begins to bleed out of it like some ghastly drool of a rabid wolf. Its hollow eyes were dark and lifeless pits with no signs of emotion. The shadow grabs the faerie with its other shadowy arm. She suddenly begins shaking in fear.

"NO!" Elfina screams, running towards the two of them. "LET HER GO!!!"

All she manages to do is go through the illusion of the two of them in front of her. She turns and watches in horror as the faerie's life gets sucked out of her body. The poor woman's face twists and screams as if she is in agonizing pain. Elfina can feel it just by being in the presence of her. The faerie then vanishes in a pile of glittering dust as what happens to faeries when they are killed.

Elfina begins to shiver and does not bother stopping the tears from falling down her cheeks. It takes all her will not to hyperventilate in panic. Instead, she goes into a cold sweat. A flash of light hits her, and she is back at the grocery market. But she is still shaking.

"Are you alright?" The stranger whispers harshly to her, not in a kindly, concerned way but in a cold, malevolent sort of way.

Elfina does not acknowledge them or even look at them. She runs past them, goes to the fastest checkout line to pay for her products and gets the hell out of there to Javas' as fast as she can.

*****

Javas stands watching the beautiful seaside from the top of the cliff. He traces his long-nailed fingers over his lengthy white beard while his deep cobalt eyes take in everything around him. The soft crashing of the waves below him, the blend of colors that melt into the sky, and the salty smell of that beachy air. Right now, Javas is wondering why the world can't be as calm as this sight is right now.

He sighs, turns away from the view and walks towards his small shed of a house. It is a solid stone hut with no real bedrooms and a small bathroom to boot. But it suits him. He is surrounded by all of his magical equipment, work, and laboratory. There is no reason for him to be without it, nor does he want to be. Not to mention that his hut is hard against every weather element known to all worlds.

When he looked into his looking glass this morning, he noticed that there was great danger coming. He has seen what had happened to these people that were struck down by these demons. Now he is very worried about it. He wipes his hands against his ancient reddish-brown robe and brushes his sandaled feet against the welcome mat that Elfina had got him for his last birthday. He steps inside his house and goes to his giant wizardry book to look up whatever this kind of demon is.

Suddenly, Javas hears his snowy owl named Voltaire wail and squeak. His white and grey feathers puff up not as a sense of danger but more of excitement. This means that he has a familiar visitor coming to see him. When Voltaire gives off another hoot, Javas waves his hand at him as a gesture to be quiet. This of course does not stop the bird. In fact, he flutters his wings and flies close to the door. He sits on the perch beside it and waits. Javas shakes his head amusedly at his feathered companion.

A knock on the doors sounds and Javas responds. "Come in."

Elfina walks in with two big bags of groceries and Javas waves her over.

"Hi Javas." Elfina greets him as she walks over to him and gives him a kiss on the cheek before putting his groceries on the only clean spot on his counter. She then puts hers on the floor beside the island he is working at.

"Ah Elfina, I have been expecting you." He speaks with a warm smile and lifts a plate of bread towards her. "Have you had your dinner?"

"Yes Javas, just before I got the groceries." She declares at him lovingly, the way a daughter loves her poor, absentminded father. Then she remembers that she has something important to tell him. "Javas, something happened to me today."

He turns from his book and looks at her with concern. He removes his glasses and pulls a stool out for her to sit on. By the look on her youthful face, Javas can tell that it is something bad. Elfina sits beside him and plants her arms on the counter. He puts a comforting hand on the arm closest to him. "Take your time, tell me what happened."

Elfina takes a deep breath, props her elbow on the table, and rests her head against it as she explains. "I think I know what is happening to these people lately. I had overheard some Valkyries talking about how Nico the vampire was killed and they mentioned that a third person. I didn't know who yet."

"Yet?" Javas interrupts with a question.

"No. It was a faerie who I have never seen before." She gives Javas a full report of what had happened to her in the market as she was getting groceries for them and the vision that she had. Javas nearly jumps out of his chair when he hears the whole story. Elfina is the closest thing he has to a daughter. The fact that he has felt this danger in the first place makes him all the more fearful for her safety.

"You didn't talk to it, did you?" Javas quickly but gently grabs her wrist as he asks her.

"No," Elfina answers putting her hand on his as she mirrors concern. "I didn't even look at it after I got that vision."

Javas lets out a sigh of relief and let's go of her wrist. "I knew that there was something going on, and now, after your description, I think I know what is causing all of this hell."

He goes back to looking at his book, and Elfina leans closer to him to read it as well. All she wants to do now is help. After he flips through the large, parchment brown pages of the book, Javas lands on a page with sharp lines forming into letters that spells out "SHADOW DEMONS" on the top of the page. Slowly, the rest of the words begin to appear on the page as regular spellings tend to on the books that wizards keep. Beside it appears a rough, dark drawing of a shadow with a jack o' lantern-like face and vicious-looking claws about to strike out. Javas puts on his tiny square glasses as Elfina moves close to Javas and puts a hand on his shoulder as he begins to read the description out loud.

"Shadow demons are supernatural specters made completely out of the darkness. Often setting out to trick their victims into believing that they are another species entirely via animal, human, or other ethereal beings. As soon as verbal contact and recognition are made, its true form, which is a black mass, is revealed. With its dark power and sociopathic relish, it will terrorize the victim and steal their essence. Therefore, killing them immediately."

"So, this is what we are up against?" Elfina asks, analyzing the danger that is before her. She turns from the book to look at her old mentor's face and hopes that he has the answers to this problem. "How do we stop it?"

"I don't know, but I promise you, my dear, I will work on it." He answers, removing his glasses and looks at her. Elfina leans her head against his shoulder. This is an old habit of hers when she sought comfort from him since she was a small child. With no one else to give her this kind of relief seeing as it was always him that took care of her. He lovingly put his hand on hers that she had looped through on his arm. "Now you told me that you did not engage this being in anyway other than bumping into him?"

Elfina looks up at him, looking desperately for some hope. "That's right."

"Well, if that is the case, this creature should leave you alone. In fact, there is a good chance that it will." Javas explains to her as he gently strokes her arm. "The worst thing you can do now my dear is be afraid. All you can truly do now is be careful and keep living your life. Remember, demons feed on our fears and anxieties. They live to ruin us by this. The best defense you have is to not worry and enjoy yourself."

Elfina smiles at him and gives him a kiss on his cheek. "Now you know that is not a problem for me."

That is the thing about Javas. He always knows how to make her feel better. And this is why she has always visited him since she was a toddler. If Elfina is being honest, he is the one who raised her since she never saw her parents that much. The only time she does is when there is some kind of harsh obligation or order that she is forced to see through. This all ended up draining her and disappointing them. She always runs to Javas, who loves her just as she is, a nymph and not some goddess that her parents continually remind her that she isn't. Javas interrupts her thoughts once again as he speaks.

"Now I believe you are going to hang?" He pauses, looking confusedly at her. "You still use that word, right? Hang?"

She gives him a bigger beam, a nod, and a chuckle as he continues. "Go hang by the beach and get some sun girl. You are looking a little too pale today. Go outside and enjoy."

With that, she stands up from the stool and joyously gives him a salute. "Yes, sir!"

Although she is planning to relax down at the beach anyway, Elfina listens to his advice and goes to his bathroom to change into her bikini. A beautiful sunny day like this should be enjoyed by being outside anyway.

*****

Elfina lays on the hot soft sand and watches the water roll with its gentle blue waves. She wonders plainly if Viola is going to come up after her shift at the bank. It would be nice to spend the rest of the afternoon with her childhood mermaid friend but Elfina understands that Viola is still a busy career woman after all. Oh well, even if she doesn't come to the surface being by the sea is a reward all on its own.

Elfina stretches out on her stomach in her leopard print bikini. As she reaches out to touch, the lukewarm velvety feel of the water caresses her fingertips. The tension that had built up from Scalars is no longer in her system. Now, she is quite content as a sweet secret smile spreads on her lips. Before she could turn over, she felt a shadow cover the sunlight on her back. With this, the nervousness creeps back into her.

It could not have followed me here, could it? Elfina spins silently in her mind. She turns to behold what is standing over her by putting up a hand to block her eyes from the harsh light.

"Gobble!" Elfina says pleasantly surprised to see the orange goldfish-looking man with big friendly eyes staring down at her. "What are you doing here?"

A wide grin appears on his equally wide face. "Just looking for any mail that needs to be delivered undersea. Missus Prudence hasn't been around too often so I am hoping that this time she has more mail for the underwater world."

He holds up his mailbag to Elfina and shows her that he has no letters of any kind to deliver.

"Understood. Do you know if Viola is going to come up to the surface today?" Elfina inquires.

A grimace crosses his face and Gobble shakes his head. "No, I don't think so. I saw her working at the bank a few moments ago and she seems to be at it very hard. Whatever it was she was doing, it doesn't look like she is getting off today."

Elfina gestures her acceptance of that. It is more than likely that Viola would be crazy busy today. "Okay, thanks Gobble. I just wanted to check."

As Elfina lays back on the beach and relaxes again, Gobble asks her in a slightly flirty manner, "Now, do you have any mail? Any shells or coral you need in your shop?"

Elfina spins to face him with a sly smile. She shakes her head at him and says coquettishly, "If you want to come by, you know that you are more than welcome to find out."

Gobble lets out a snicker, gives her a wave goodbye and waddles himself back into the sea. A large, loud splash hits the water in the distance as he dives back underwater, returning to his duties. Seeing this, Elfina props herself up on her feet. With full responsibility and spontaneity, she darts into the sea and dives head first into the water.

The luxurious feel of the liquid surrounding her entire body cleanses her mind, body, and soul in one swoop. She feels her heart open up and feel lighter than it had her that whole afternoon. Her soul is feeling freer than a butterfly with both sensations of hot and cold press against her skin. With her skin being warm from the sun and the water being so breezy, it is like she has a cool force field enveloping her. Not one to give up an impulse of any kind, Elfina swims around the water in her own freewheeling style. No matter what happens in the future, she wants nothing more than to live in this moment.

*****

Outside of her home, Elfina sits on the tree branch that sits just outside of her bedroom window, watching the vibrant twilight in the sky. Dressed in her comfy blue sweats, Elfina reads the latest romance novel that has just come out on the market. She loves these novels because they always have a happy ending, and Elfina knows that she can not function without a happy ending to a story. Although she is only mid-way through her chapter, Elfina sets the book down and looks to the sunset.

She would never tell anyone, not even her closest friends, but she too longs for love. Something real, a mate. A person to share both the sunrises and sunsets with. It is not without trying. Elfina knows that she flirts a lot, but so do all nymphs and just because she flirts does not mean she is promiscuous in any way, just playful. She has always chosen the men she dates with the utmost care. Sure, she would give a man a chance and get to know him. However, if she was going to share her body with him, she wanted to be sure that he was the kind of person worth sharing herself with first. Despite the flirty, self-possessed mask that she wears, all she wants is true love.

"I do wear it oh so well." She thinks smiling and chuckling to herself.

Just like what Stephan and Jacqueline have. She has a feeling that when she meets her true love it would be love at first sight. It would be unwise and unconditional because that is her when it comes to love of any kind. Her problem is that she wants a sure thing and sadly, lots of love stories are not like that at all. She just has to look at the divorce rates in the Earth Realm to know that's true.

Looking out at the sunset, Elfina enjoys the view she has right now and focuses on that. The bright colors of the sun and sky blend in perfect harmony. It is like watching a true love story happening right before her eyes. With thoughts of love and gratitude filling her mind, Elfina remembers what a truly wonderful world she lives in, even if it isn't always easy. There are some scary things happening right now, but if you know where to look, you can see the beauty of it.

Elfina indulges in a happy sigh, opens her book, and begins to read the pages where she had left off. She plans to finish it, hopefully before the sun goes completely down. Whether she does or not is immaterial to her. She just wants to take in the romance of all that is happening around her.

Chapter Six

The sun rises, shining brightly through Elfina's window. The rays dance sweetly on her sleepy face as she lays fast asleep on her pink petal-like bed. She scrunches up her face as she feels the light through her eyes. Not even opening her eyes, she rubs her face on her white pillow to keep the brightness of the sun away for a little longer. In a few seconds, she opens her eyes towards her arched window and smiles as she feels the warm light on her face. With no desire to get out of her soft, comfy bed, she presses her fingers to her lips to blow the sun a kiss. Without meaning to, she rolls over, falling onto the cushions that she keeps on the floor. Elfina always forgets that there isn't a bed there and too many times she falls out of bed. At least she has something soft to land on. But still, she does not want to get up.

A push off her pillows has her picking herself up. Her eyes trail proudly around her bedroom as it reflects her personal style. She knows this as she looks around with her sleepy eyes and smiles with contentment. The room is round and the walls are the wood of the tree that she inhabits. The curtains over her window are vivid grass green chiffon curtains with a small end table that holds a crystal ball that sits on a gold-colored metal holder with swirls adorning it. On the floor before her spiraling staircase, a round deep cobalt Persian rug sits like a wayward puddle after a rainstorm. Beside the staircase is her closet, which is filled with the items of clothing that she has carefully chosen and absolutely loves. Candles of every color sat on every surface in her room, while a silver antique dish that sits on her nightstand contains crystals and gemstones. She has as many gems as she does of the candles. The only difference between the candles and the gems is that the gems are just in that one spot. It gives her a chuckle knowing this contrast. She looks at the blue-green dreamcatcher that she hangs over her bed, knowing that even now, it is still doing its job of keeping the bad dreams away. Her eyes look to her glass suncatchers with the light through it shining a rainbow of colors on her walls. These walls were adorned with pictures of flowers, fairies, and butterflies.

Elfina walked over to her vanity table to collect the white flowing silk robe that sat on her cushioned stool. As she gazes into her small vanity mirror, she slips her robe over her shoulders. On this small table, she has her perfume, make-up, and the music box made of shells that Viola had given to her for her birthday. As she does every morning, Elfina opens the box and listens to the gentle tune as she sits on her stool. She runs a brush through her hair, thinking about what kind of quote would suit her mood right now. Suddenly, she thinks the old tried and true "Keep calm and carry on" is the one.

She gets up and walks down her stairs straight into the small kitchen that she has. This is where her little herb boxes sit on her window sill, pots hang on a metal pot rack that sits beside her stove, and the walls are a light cheerful yellow that she had painted herself. With a smile, Elfina treads towards the cupboard with a purple pansy painted on it and opens it.

There she selects one of her mismatched coffee mugs and on the shelf above them, picks up a tin with a white flower on the label. This is her jasmine green tea, and it is what she wants to drink first thing this morning. She always drinks some kind of green tea, but this morning requires something a little more. She puts water in her kettle from the sink, walks over to her stove, turns the knob, and places the kettle gently on the stove before walking to the refrigerator to get her breakfast.

A couple of whole wheat slices of bread with margarine and honey sit on a plate in front of her. Her kettle boils and she rushes to the stove to retrieve it. She pours the boiling water into her coffee pot which is in the shape of a pink rose with a spout. The sound of a knock at her front door rings in her ears. She wrinkles her face in confusion.

"I'm not expecting anyone." She speaks silently to herself. Elfina walks to her door and sees Viola on the other side of it wearing a trim primrose blue suit.

"Viola!" Elfina says with surprise and happily gives her best friend a hug. Viola returns the hug and gives Elfina a friendly peck on the cheek.

"Hi Elfina," she cheerfully replies as they break apart from the hug. "I hear you were at the beach yesterday. I'm sorry we could not hang out."

"No worries." Elfina says as she steps aside to let Viola pass through her front door. "Come in hon! I am just having some breakfast."

Following her friend into the kitchen, Viola straightens out her skirt before she sits on one of the stools at the small island. She watches Elfina brush some margarine onto some bread slices with a butter knife.

"Would you like some breakfast too?" Elfina turns and looks to her friend.

"No, but I'll have some coffee if you are making some."

"Sure, my dear."

With great cheer, Elfina strides herself to the cabinet with a daisy painted on it and grabs the coffee percolator that she keeps for the company that likes the stuff. She plugs it into her wall and puts some freshly grinded beans into it. Although she never liked coffee, Elfina kept it on hand, especially when at least five people she knows love the stuff. Viola is one of those people, but luckily, she is a woman who doesn't want anything fancy done with it. She likes things that are simple and organized with no frills. Elfina brings her the coffee and sits across from her on the other stool.

After sipping some of her own tea, Elfina pipes up, "So what's happening? Are you speaking up at the university again?"

"No." Viola answers, sipping her coffee. "I just thought I would come and see you before you head off to your store."

"That's nice but don't you have to work today?"

"No, not really but I do have a lunch date this afternoon."

With an excited whoop, Elfina puts a hand on her friend's and gives it a light pat. "That's great! I'm so thrilled for you. You will have to tell me all about it."

"I will but I wanted to check on you first." In a nervous gesture, Viola starts to wring her hands. Elfina is happy that her friend is going to go on a date again. Not since that professor has, she had a date in a few years that isn't work related in anyway. There is hope for her yet. Viola is a shy woman especially when it comes to romance. But Elfina is always happy to give her friend that boost of confidence she needs whether it is a pep-talk or advice.

In this case, Viola is not nervous about the date. When she came to the surface and waited for her legs to emerge from her tail, Javas was waiting for her and told her something. Elfina has this sense too which is why she speaks up.

"When did you see Javas?"

Viola looks to Elfina with her eyes wide in surprise. She can not help but be astonished that her friend could sense this from her. Elfina lifts her eyebrows and gives her friend an amused nod as if to say, "I can read you like a book." With a sigh, Viola confesses. "When I came to the surface and was waiting to shed my fins."

Before Elfina lifts her tea to her lips she hears her toaster ring. "Woah!" She lets out of her mouth and nearly drops her teacup on the table. Viola watches Elfina pull her toast out of the appliance. Clearly, it is very hot when she sees her friend flinch and shake her hand before sucking on her fingers. However, when she sees that Elfina is being all too silent, she could not shake the feeling that her friend is unhappy with her. She has to rectify that.

"Don't be mad, Sweetie. I'm just really concerned about you. After all, you are my best friend and I want you to be safe." Viola says and Elfina turns to face her.

She sits beside her friend again and starts to butter her toast. Then she spreads honey on it and looks back to her friend with a smile. "I'm not mad Honey. In fact, I consider myself lucky that I have some many wonderful people who care about me the way that you all do." Elfina searches Viola's face and can see that her concern is still there and not lifting anytime soon. She takes a bite of her toast and continues. "But the best thing I can do and Javas said this too is that I have to go on living my life. I will not be afraid and press on with good cheer. I have faith that everything will be alright."

After her last statement, Elfina notices Viola's face looking a little less stressed and a lot more hopeful. Her expression seems a little more serene with her small smile and quiet eyes. Elfina lifts her teacup to her friend, and Viola does the same with hers. They clink each other's cups and take a sip of their respective hot drinks.

Viola studies Elfina as she eats her breakfast. She admires how her friend is so fearless like she is never afraid of anything. She does not know how she does it. Her self-confidence is so inspiring, yet it is lacking in Viola. She knows this and accepts it, never hating herself for it. Viola has learned to be content with what she has. Besides, there is enough feistiness and vivacity in her friends that she did not need to add anymore to the pile.

Viola smiles at her friend and continues to sip her coffee, "I'm glad to hear that. Just promise me that you are going to be careful, okay?"

"Okay." Elfina nods at her.

"And if something does happen, you will call me straight away? No hesitation or doubts. Just call me." Viola says as she finds herself relaxing more on her stool.

"I promise you I will. Don't worry about me, Sweetie. I think everything will turn out for the best in the end." With the last sip of her tea, Elfina walks towards her staircase. "Now, while I change into some real clothes, you can tell me all about this man you are going to see. I suggest we all go out to dinner tonight as well."

"Sounds great." Viola says as she finishes her coffee and follows her friend up the stairway. When she reaches the top, Elfina turns and looks at her friend. "I guarantee you that we will all want details about this mystery date."

Viola shakes her head at Elfina and snickers at her. The two of them continue to her room to try and find the perfect outfit for the day. Who knows what it is going to bring?

*****

Later on, that day, Elfina sits in her office working on her sales books. She goes through every numerical figure that she could on a page, feeling her eyes begin to blur more and more. Each number seems to make her head spin, and it is annoying. *Oh well,* Elfina thinks to herself and shakes her head. This is just a minor annoyance that a life of freedom is going to throw at her. She knows that she has to take the good with the bad. Sometimes the bad gives her the bite that she needs in order to appreciate what good she does have.

Reminding herself of this, she takes a deep breath, shakes her head, and gets back to work. By the look of these figures, her store did pretty well today. She did have a steady stream of customers and they all bought at least one item. When she sees that most people today purchased an aromatherapy item of some kind, she has to chuckle. It looks like scents are the hip thing right about now.

She looks up from her parchment scrolls as soon as she hears a knock on her front door. Mystification crosses on her face as she wonders who this could be. She has her closed signup and everything, and is she expecting any shipments to be delivered now? With a sigh, Elfina stands up from her desk and decides to see who is there and what they could want.

As soon as she stands up, Elfina feels a heaviness on her shoulder that could only mean bad vibes are present. This is not normal for her; she wouldn't feel like this unless… She grabs her office doorknob and feels a strong premonition hit her. She no longer sees her office door but the outside of her shop. Standing at the front door is a shadowy mist that immediately makes her sick to her stomach. It does nothing but just float there. However, Elfina could feel how dangerous this thing is just by being aware of it. A pair of red glowing eyes appear on top of it. They stare into her as if they want to rip her to shreds.

"I want you." She hears this shadow whisper in a low, sinister growl. "I want your body. I want your soul; I want your LIFE!"

Elfina's skin grows cold as its evil words spread fear throughout her body, like tiny icicles piercing into her blood. In mere seconds, she finds herself back in her office facing her door. After seeing this vision and getting all these negative feelings, Elfina knows that this could only mean one thing. That this demon is at her shop door, trying to get in. She doesn't think this anymore. She knows it.

She has to get out of here. Looking around, there is no way she could run out of here in this form and escape this parasite safely. Suddenly, she has an idea, and it is crazy enough to work. Elfina forces herself to be calm like the river waters or at the beach where the ocean gently presses onto the sand. She sees this with her mind's eye. Her body slowly transforms into a clear liquid, just like the water a person would see in a fountain. In a matter of minutes her whole body is morphed into a puddle.

She seeps herself through the cracks in her wooden floorboards and soaks herself into the soil. As fast as she can Elfina travels through the ground looking for the pipes that go into Meira's workshop. She has to find them or she knows that she is a goner. But that is not what her mind is on. She just hopes that this horrible creature does not follow her to her friend's place. She would never forgive herself if she put someone she loves in danger. However, if she is not alone then this thing could not hurt either one of them. Meira is her only hope now for safety.

Finally, for what seems like an eternity, Elfina finds the pipe that she is looking for. She spreads herself around the small connector of the pipe, looking for any small opening she can find. In two minutes, she seeps herself into the pipe and floats her way towards Meira's sink.

Meira is in her shop pounding hard with her hammer on the sword she is working on. Clank, clank, clank, she continues to hit it rhythmically and feels the sweat drip from her brow. She brushes her dirt-covered brow with the back of her gloved hand and lets out a weary sigh. She sets her hammer and sword down on the ground, feeling the fatigue of a hard day's work take her over.

"Perhaps I should stop here." Meira says to herself.

She stands up from her stool and makes her way towards her workshop sink which is a lot dirtier than she is at that moment. Meira turns on the faucet and lets the cool waterfall onto the palms of her cupped hands. Quickly she splashes her face with it until something feels odd. She cracks her eyes open and can see that what is falling onto her hands is not water at all but something else. It looks like water but feels warm and viscous like a mould of clear clay. She drops whatever it is on her hands and watches it take form in front of her eyes. The odd liquid takes on the shape of someone she knows very well.

"Elfina!" Meira yells in surprise and runs to her friend who is squatting inside her sink shivering. Meira runs to her and puts her hands on her arms in alarm. After the initial shock wears off, her natural sarcasm hits. "You know, most people use a door, even the ghosts."

"Most people don't have a shadow demon at their front door," Elfina replies in a shaky voice. Seeing the fear on her friend's face, Meira helps her out of the sink.

With Elfina still shaking from the combination of cold water and fearful happenings, she recounts what happened to her to Meira. Meira already knows about what happened to her at Scalars where she bumped into the entity but didn't talk to him. This news was sent to both her and Ozzie via crystal call. Both nymph and elf go into Meira's apartment, and she grabs a dry, clean towel to wrap it around a shaking Elfina.

"I tell you Elfina, only you know how to attract the biggest freakizoids." Meira says, rubbing her friend's arms trying to get her warm again. Elfina lets out a laugh that sounds suspiciously like a cry. This causes Meira to embrace her friend and give her some comfort. "Come into the kitchen and I'll make you a tea to warm you up. There is a dragon chai with your name on it."

Elfina nods and brushes the tears out of her eyes. She follows Meira into her kitchen and the two of them put the kettle on the stove. Meira turns and looks to Elfina, holding her arms gently again. "You're sure it didn't follow you?"

"I'm sure," Elfina says feeling the calm wash over her, thanks to the warmness she feels with this towel. "I would have sensed it, and so would you."

"Okay but you are alright?" Meira asks her with concern and without a trace of humour.

"Yes." Elfina nods as genuine regret starts to cling to her heart. "I'm sorry Meira. I don't want to put you in danger. I was just so afraid."

"No, no, no." Meira says with a kindly and comforting tone which she only reserves for the people that she is truly close to. "You should have. Whatever this thing is, you can not face it yourself. This thing is already dangerous and it is moving fast. Did you know that since the pixie, it has killed two more people? The Knights and Valkyries are going through hell trying to catch these creatures."

The two of them sit at the kitchen table as Meira brings over two cups of hot tea. She places one in front of Elfina and one in front of herself. As Elfina begins to sip the spicy, tepid tea, Meira tells her something important.

"I've been hearing some things from the crystal balls lately hon." Meira begins. Elfina looks at her friend and listens closely. "The authorities believe that it is more than one demon now. They are saying that it is at least three or four. The psychic team has found that out. There was also some black slime residue. These demons are attacking at random and no one is safe right now."

"This is a frightening turn of events." Elfina chimes in, sipping her tea. "So, what should I do now then?"

"You shouldn't be alone, Sweetie," Meira says caringly putting her hand on Elfina's. "Just be careful. We can't leave everything up to the Knights and Valkyries."

"What do you think should be done?" Elfina asks.

Taking in a deep sigh, Meira brings her hand back to her cup and answers. "Well continue to live your life just as Javas told you so. But as soon as you sense that something is wrong like you did today, you come to one of us. Me, Jacqueline, or Viola. Just come so we know you are okay and can be somewhat safe."

"Yes, I promise you that I will," Elfina says as she stands up from her chair, puts her teacup in the sink, and sets her towel down on her chair. She looks over at her normally cynical friend and can feel the worry come off of her in waves. Determined to make everything alright again Elfina decides to help stop her friend from fretting. Elfina continues. "Now let's go out to dinner. We have got to figure out how Viola's date went."

A hint of a smile appears on Meira's face and Elfina goes to the stainless-steel tea kettle to look at her reflection. Her make-up has run and her hair is tangled. Luckily, Meira comes up behind her with a hairbrush and a wet cloth. In a matter of minutes, Elfina fixes her make-up and her wild hair looks like it usually does.

"Am I dry enough?" Elfina asks looking at Meira.

"You look great and I agree. Let's go out before I starve myself into nothing."

With some chatter and giggles, Elfina and Meira leave the apartment and head out to meet up with the rest of the girls for their dinner. To their minds, good food and even better company always fix bad situations even if you were nearly a shadow demon's latest victim.

*****

88

At the Black Dragon Pub, four friends sit at their favourite table enjoying their chosen drinks and appetizers, along with a good portion of gossip.

"Come on Viola! You promised to tell us about this mystery lunch date you went on." Jacqueline chimes in as she sips her cow's blood from her giant glass goblet. Her brow arches as she gets a wicked idea forming in her brain. "Or are you just embarrassed because you had a lunchtime quickie too?"

Viola begins to shake her head while her natural blush rises in her cheeks. "Oh, Jacqueline! No! We did not have sex." She says flabbergasted but, in her mind, she reminds herself that she should not be surprised as this is what her friends are like. So, she gives an answer. "But this one does have some potential."

"Alright! Now we are getting somewhere." Meira nods as she takes a sip of her beer. "What's he like?"

"Smart, sweet, and he loves his job." Viola says with a delightful little twinkle in her dark brown eyes.

"Well, he is a man of integrity. That is a good thing." Elfina says with a smile not quite reaching her eyes. "Are you going to see him again?"

"If he comes around again," Viola says looking playfully fluttering her eyelashes at her friend. "I would not say no to date number two."

"Good." Jacqueline says giving her young mermaid friend a wicked grin. "But if he mistreats you. Let us know."

With a giggle and a blush, Viola puts a hand to her face hoping that she is hiding it. "Don't worry. I'll let you know but if he is that bad, you know I'll break his legs."

"That's the spirit!" Jacqueline toasts her goblet in the air. "Cheers everyone! Here's to keeping good men honest."

A series of laughs have all four women clinking their glasses to each other and finishing the toast with a sip.

"So Elfina." Viola says hoping to change the subject to anything else. "How was work today? Did you stay out of trouble?"

After that question, Elfina's face falls, and she looks towards Meira whose concern starts to show on her as well. The two of them realize that they must tell Jacqueline and Viola everything. The vampire and mermaid both already know about everything that happened up until the incident at the marketplace. But this is a dangerous situation that has just happened only a couple of hours ago. Elfina just does not want to spoil any kind of cheer that is to be had thanks to this incident.

Elfina takes a deep breath in and confesses. "Actually, I do have to tell you guys something."

She tells Jacqueline and Viola everything that happened from when she had her premonition to her daring escape to Meira's. Wide-eyed worry is easily seen on both her undead and siren friends' faces. With both of their mouths open and drinks forgotten, they just stare at her. Their friend's clairvoyance is never wrong. It can be confusing when it comes across as a riddle but it is never wrong. The fact that her gift is warning her of this impending doom is the cherry on top of this whole mess.

"It was very scary," Meira tells the rest of the group. "She came through my sink in a state of terror. Not that I blame her."

"Oh dear. What happens now Elfina?" Viola asks with heavy concern tracing in her voice.

"I don't think anything just yet." She replies after taking a generous sip of her wine. "It hasn't attacked me yet and I haven't directly acknowledged it yet. So hopefully things will be getting better."

"Sweetie." Jacqueline says as she turns to face Elfina and puts a gentle somewhat motherly hand on her arm. "Take it from someone who is considered demonic. They don't give up those demons. If they can find ways to get in and hurt you, they will."

"Yes, you see," Meira says shaking her head and giving a funny half smile. "I always tell you that you attract the wrong kind of men, but do you listen to me? No!"

Meira shakes her head and gives a playfully wicked smile on her face that earns a laugh from the group sitting at the table. Elfina wipes a laughter tear away from her left eye before piping up.

"Yeah, but if I do start to listen to you, then you'd know that I have problems."

"Oh, cute! You always were a saucy nutter." Meira says and they all laugh out loud again. Elfina looks to Meira and sends her a silent thanks for bringing a sense of light-heartedness back to the situation. She returns Elfina's nod and taps her goblet to hers. It is true that there isn't anything Meira wouldn't do to fix a nasty situation, especially when humour needs to be involved.

"And here I thought you would never notice that," Elfina says to her playfully. "It's about time."

"Speaking of time, what time is it?" Jacqueline asks, looking around the room for a clock. "Stephan should be back from hunting with his pack right around now."

"You are going to *howl* at the moon with him tonight, Jacqueline?" Elfina gives Jacqueline a wink and a naughty look.

Jacqueline returns Elfina's wicked look with her own. "Honey, you may have a beast that needs a good hanging, but I have a beast at home that needs a good shagging."

Jacqueline gives a slap to her black-cladded bottom. A loud "ow!" escapes all the women's lips and they let out a laugh. With that all four women stand up and embrace each other. Jacqueline approaches Elfina and gives her a kiss on each cheek before embracing her.

"If anything does happen. Please scream as loud as you can to me with your head, and I'll be there in a flash."

"I will Jacqueline. And thank you so much." Elfina whispers back and breaks the embrace.

"My pleasure, my dear." Jacqueline turns and looks at the rest of her friends. "Good night girls. It certainly is a beautiful one for sure."

Without another word, Jacqueline slinks away to the door. The three of them watch her go and giggle as they make their own way towards the exit. Viktor walks towards their table to clear up their finished plates. He had heard every word, and that's why his face is fallen right now. He watches the remaining three leave and feels his heart shatter at the thought of one of them being stalked by this demon.

Carrying the tray full of dirty dishes in his hands, he walks into the kitchen. After he drops the dishes in the sink, he mutters a silent spell. The dishes leap into the air as if invisible hands are moving them. Brushes and sponges lather themselves up and wash the dishes thoroughly. Viktor sighs and walks over to his wife, Madeline who is stirring the shepherd's stew with a large wooden spoon.

"Hi, Maddy." He says as he puts his arms around her plump waist and buries his face in her wild hair. In this one rare instance, she does not want to whack him with her spoon as she senses the anxiety in her husband. "One of our favorite patrons is in trouble. Tomorrow I will talk to the Knights and Valkyries, then go speak to Javas. There has to be something we can do."

"Indeed, Viktor. Just this once you get no argument from me." The wrinkled face of Maddy showed a great deal of concern. "They are good girls but I too have sensed great danger."

*****

When the four women reach the entrance to Mystina Forest, Meira turns to face her friends. "Good night girls. Be safe." She pauses for a brief moment and looks at Elfina. She walks to her and puts her arms around her, pulling her into a friendly embrace. "You too Elfina, please be careful."

Knowing that it is rare for Meira to show this much concern, Elfina returns the hold. "I will."

Satisfied with that answer, Meira breaks from the hug and walks towards her own home. Elfina and Viola walk into the brilliant forest with its multiple hues in silence. Viola looks to Elfina, no longer able to keep her concerns to herself. She pipes up.

"Are you sure you don't want me to stay with you, Sweetie? I don't like the thought of you being alone."

"I'll be alright," Elfina says, stopping her friend and putting a reassuring hand on her folded arms. "They cannot hurt me unless I invite them in. I'll message you first thing in the morning. Okay?"

Viola takes a gentle but deep breath in, feeling both helpless and unhappiness in knowing that Elfina is right about that. She reluctantly agrees as she nods her head at Elfina. The two of them continue to walk towards Elfina's house. When Elfina climbs up to the stoop of her doorway, Viola stops at the bottom of the stairs. She looks at Elfina, and her frightened eyes tell Elfina everything.

"Hey!" Elfina says, holding her hand out for her friend's. "I'm going to be fine."

Viola nods, and Elfina hops down from the stoop to give her friend a reassuring clasp. The two of them break from the quick hug and face each other.

"Good night, Sweetie." Elfina chirps up cheerfully. "I'll talk to you tomorrow."

"Be sure you do because I don't want to be fretting about you forever, you know," Viola says with a half-smile, trying to channel her inner Elfina and make light of the situation.

A snort escapes Elfina's mouth as she walks inside her house. Viola turns and happily travels towards the ocean, feeling that no matter how awkward it comes off, she succeeds in being funny.

While she is inside, Elfina decides to take precautions and locks her door. She never had to do it before but she can agree with all of her friends that she has to be extra cautious right now. With a loud click of the door, Elfina lets out a breath and turns towards her staircase. She presses her back to her door and, without meaning allows her anxiety to grow inside of her.

She closes her eyes and presses her fingers lightly to her eyes. With a shake of her head and a harsh grunt, Elfina looks to her stairwell and makes a decision. She is going to go have a nice long hot bath before she turns in for the night. The thought of some lavender salt scrub is just what she needs right now. With all of this crazy demonic crap happening, she needs a little self-care.

Shaking off her anxiety, Elfina slowly walks up her staircase, picturing her worries disappearing with each step that she takes. She will not let whatever this blackhearted demon is destroy her life even if it chases her all over the Nether Realm. At the top of her staircase, she looks into her bathroom which is just next to her bedroom.

Inside, it is filled with blues, shells, sand-colored towels and matts. She wanted her bathroom to look like a beach and that is what she got. She lets out a relaxed breath and walks over to her white clawfoot tub. She turns her silver-toned taps and lets the water run while dusting her chosen salts into the tub. Then, sitting on her tray, she looks at the essential oils that she keeps on them. A dash of camomile, a drop of mint, and a little extra lavender will hit the spot. Elfina smiles at the oils and is happy to have this knowledge of them.

While watching the oils blend softly into the water, Elfina strips out of her sundress and lets it fall to the floor. She switches off the taps and continues to remove all of her undergarments. She stands at the edge of the tub completely naked, steps lightly into the hot pool of water, and the shock of it has her inhale sharply through her teeth. After she feels herself getting used to the temperature, Elfina places her other leg in and finds it less of a shock.

Slowly, Elfina lowers her whole body into the tub and feels the heat touch each part of her skin that she allows it to. As her body melts into the tub, she relaxes more and more. Her eyes close and she lets the soothing heat take her wherever it wants to. She allows herself to sink deeper into the water until she is completely submerged. Yes. This did the trick and now her worries are deliberately washing away.

*****

A black mist forms itself outside of the nymph's treehouse. It has been watching since the siren had walked away from the treehouse. This little quaint cottage with its sweet round windows and spots of color is about to get engulfed in darkness. Hidden in the bush is the shadow demon and it wants this shining happiness little victim all to itself. It imagined that her life force must taste like sunshine and wild berries.

It is difficult because this one is never alone, but she is now. It may be a challenge, but that is what makes this so much more titillating. Besides, it will not give up. It never will. Like a predator that hunts for its quick and clever prey, it will stalk her until the right moment.

The lust it has for this wonderful little nymph could never be sated by another. It will find a way to trick her into letting it in. There is nowhere for her to run or hide when it enters into her own domain. Even if she left, it will always come for her to devour her is not just going to be satisfying but it is going to be a pleasure.

It could not wait for her any longer. It whisks itself towards the front door at a speed that would have the fastest imp tremble. Nothing will keep it from getting what it wants. It wants her blood. It wants to view the life slowly seeping out of her lithe little body. And when she goes limp in its tentacles, the need to kill would be fulfilled…for now.

Chapter Seven

Back at the Moon Tower, where a small part of this massive structure contains a big room, a big BEDROOM to be exact. It is a chamber that is considered to be luxurious to most vampires due to its classical architecture and decor. It has a gothic feel with its high ceilings and equally tall windows with a balcony that faces to the east. It is the perfect way to keep an eye on the moon. A fire is going in the fireplace and lying on a bed of rose red velvet sheets is Jacqueline, reading a small book on time travel. Wearing a long silk gown that matches the glow of the moon, she waits for her husband, who is in the bathroom, taking a shower. The hunt with his pack went well, or so she imagines since she had seen him work up a good sweat from running through the forest for most of the night when he walked in.

"Are you alright in there?" She calls out to him.

"Yeah. I'm just getting the rest of that deer out of my teeth." He replies as he strolls into the room in nothing but his striped pajama pants. As he wipes his freshly shaven face, she gazes over to him, smiling. She sets her book on her golden-plated nightstand.

"How sexy, darling." Jacqueline purrs out to him in a somewhat sinister but seductive kind of way as she trails her foot up and down a long silk-leaden leg. She desires to give him a little signal and taking the hint he smiles as he struts over to her.

Stephan sits beside her, leans in, and presses his slightly furred mouth to her beautiful red lips. Whenever he kisses his wife, Stephan feels himself sinking into a dream. He runs his strong, callused hands gently up her milk-white arms. Slowly, he lifts his head up to look into her foggy grey eyes.

"I love you. You do know that, don't you?" He whispers sweetly to her.

"Of course, but don't ever stop reminding me." She murmurs back, wrapping her arms around his neck.

She brings him close as he trails a hand down her night dress and begins to lift the material from her thigh. Completely intoxicated, Stephan trails his lips along her jaw as Jacqueline's fangs appear. A vampire's fangs always surface when they have powerful feelings or urges. With their mouths pressing together in a deep, intense kiss, Jacqueline binds her legs around his waist and prepares herself for the love they have shared for centuries.

*****

Elfina sits, tucked in her bed, adorned in a lovely white cotton nightgown, and reads a book called, "Adventures in Atlantis" rather than that time travel non-fiction that Jacqueline is currently reading. As she trails her eyes across the words, she thinks how amazing it would be to see Atlantis again. It is such a beautiful island, and maybe she should vacation there again. It is famous for being one of the Nether Realm's top resorts, with its palm trees, aquamarine beaches, and sexy selkie boys. Yes, she will definitely have to vacation there again and soon.

Elfina lets out a large yawn and reaches out towards her ceiling indulging in a big stretch. After she puts her book down on her glittering tiled nightstand, Elfina sways over to turn off her lamp when suddenly it goes off by itself. Slightly confused, Elfina leaves her arm reaching for the lamp in midair for a couple of seconds. She shrugs her shoulders before she lays back on her bed, deciding that the electrical storm in her lamp must have fused out. With her index fingers, she rubs her temples and drifts off to sleep. Before she could fall completely into a dream state, the lamp suddenly flicks back on. She gradually looks back at the lamp to study it. It is like it didn't even fuse out. Shaking her head she reaches for it again and watches it snuff out again. She keeps her eyes on her lamp and the more she watches it the more befuddled she becomes. When it turns back on again, she finds her nerves on a high level as it keeps flickering on and off, faster and faster, over and over.

Unexpectedly, she hears a noise that has her leap out of her bed and lands hard on her pillowed floor. The evillest laugh fills the bedroom like a small mocking childing pulling the wings off of a tortured fly. In a state of terror, she finds herself scrambling up off the floor and reversing her steps until her back is up against the wall. As the laugh echoes throughout the room and the lamp keeps turning on and off with a vengeance, Elfina puts her hands over her ears to drown out the evil-sounding laugh, but to no avail.

The whole room begins to shake as if an earthquake has suddenly hit. Elfina runs towards the stairs and holds on to the railing for dear life as she stumbles down the stairs with the whole house shaking. Just as fast as it started, it stopped. The laughter, the shaking, everything just stops. Elfina shakily walks towards her living room, where her popozon chair which is filled with colourful pillows and bookshelves along the walls, resides.

She carefully steps into the room, towards her chair when a single book flies off the shelf straight in her direction. One at a time more books fly off the shelf at her. She covers her head and runs to the other corner of the room to get away from the shelves. All of her books fly around the room as Elfina helplessly watches and waits for them all to fly at her again. Instead, they all stop and hover in the middle of her room like they are frozen in time.

Eyes wide with shock, a scratching noise outside of her house on the window gets her attention. At the window there are two glowing red eyes peering in at her. These red eyes are menacing, but a melodious voice starts to ring in her mind.

"Please let me in." The emotionless yet hypnotic voice speaks in a gentle manner. "I can help you. I will save you from the demon inside your house."

It is trying to fool her! Elfina shot the violent eyes a look of being insulted. She will not allow herself to be fooled by this creature. With all the strength of her mind, Elfina closes her eyes, holds onto her head again, and screams for Jacqueline.

*****

In her bed after a night of good sex, Jacqueline is sprawled out naked next to Stephan with his arm around her shoulders. With a few silent murmurs and satisfied pleasures, Stephan starts to kiss her shoulder and makes his way up to her neck when she abruptly hears Elfina's voice shrieking in her head.

"Jacqueline!!! Help me!!! It's here! Help me!!"

She sits up quickly in a cold sweat with a worried look written across her face. She continues to hear her friend's frantic pleas for help. Stephan sits up as well, holding onto his wife as he desperately studies her face. He looks to find any sign that she is okay.

"My love! What is it?"

"It's Elfina," Jacqueline says fearfully and gets up off the bed. In her rush, she grabs her robe to dress herself. "She's in trouble! I have got to go."

After hearing this, Stephan jumps out of bed himself. He grabs some pants and puts them on, "I'll follow, and I'll bring the pack."

Jacqueline doesn't argue. She just acts as she bursts through the French doors of her balcony, running barefoot on its cold stones. With her fangs bared, she calls into the night. The screech a vampire makes is that of a bat that can be heard at great distances and echoes in every direction. Bats come from every direction as they surround her, and she disappears into them. In a matter of seconds, the swarm travel with her in the direction of Mystina Forest.

Stephan on the other hand, ruptures through the front entrance of the tower. He looks up to the moon and lets out a summoning howl. With the screaming at his painful transformation, fur grows out of every pore in his skin while his ears and eyes morph into that of a wolf's. His face distorts into a long snout and his teeth grow just as fast as his claws. Other members of his pack join him as soon as his wolf form is complete.

He sets off to run through the Dark Forest with the rest of the pack trailing after him.

As Jacqueline and her swarm of bats head into the forest where Elfina's home is, the demonic black mist still haunts her through the window. It can still see her cowering in the corner but it is more confused than enraged that she has not let it in yet. Then again emotions other than fear is baffling to a demon. A slight squint of its red eyes only lasts for a few seconds before it chooses to let out another evil laugh to threaten the shuddering nymph. However, it does not get the chance. In its twisted brain, it senses something. A presence that is just as clouded as its own is making its way here. It turns and faces the sky when the sound of screeching bats gets louder. It realizes now that it is temporarily foiled. A curse emits from its jagged mouth as the dark being disintegrates into the air.

On the ground in the front yard, the bats disappear, and Jacqueline appears with her werewolf husband not far behind. With a few barks from Stephan, the pack separates from each other to scour and search the property. He trots up to his wife. The wolf looks up at her and quickly becomes a man again.

"Is she okay?" He asks with concern, "The pack is checking the area. Whatever is here, it could not have gone far."

"I have yet to check on her." Jacqueline declares with worry as she runs to her friend's door.

"I'll stay out here to make sure that everything is safe."

Jacqueline turns from her husband to the door and starts knocking desperately. "Elfina! Elfina!" She repeats over and over, praying that everything is alright.

Elfina is still crouching down on the floor and holding her head as if she has a terrible agonizing headache. With tears streaming down her face, she hears the sound of Jacqueline's voice. Without a second thought Elfina races to the door to let her in. When Jacqueline comes in, she finds that Elfina is shaking and that scares her. Jacqueline holds onto her terrified friend and strokes her hair to try and comfort her.

"You're not hurt are you honey?" She questions her friend just as she calms down. Elfina's only reply is by shaking her head. "Okay," Jacqueline pauses to only pull away and look at her friend. "Here's what we will do. I'll call the rest of the gang plus our good ol' civil servants. It's time they got involved with this."

Elfina knows that it is the right thing to do. She bows her head and points Jacqueline towards her crystal ball so that she can make the calls to the others.

*****

Within fifteen minutes, Elfina's house is filled with her friends and the knights. Elfina is sitting in her chair in front of the empty bookcase while her friends are sitting in various spots around her, wherever there isn't a mess of books.

The five knights each took a different room. They all spend a good amount of time thoroughly searching their way through their assigned rooms. One knight is opening all the cupboards in the kitchen while another is in her living room on his hands and knees, looking under the bookshelf. One of the knights walks to Elfina's door and brings in an ethereal-looking psychic who is clearly there to find the demon's hiding spot. As that knight leads the psychic to the staircase, another knight approaches Elfina and her friends.

"Well, it is a shadow demon and it is gone for now but we will find this thing." He speaks with a wave of his hand which causes a floating parchment paper and a feather-quilled pen to appear in the air. After he gives a second wave at it with his iron-gloved hand, the quill goes to the paper to start the notes. He looks towards Elfina. "Now Miss, can you tell me what happened."

Elfina doesn't hesitate to answer. "Well, I was lying in bed when the electric storm in my lamp kept flickering on and off. I didn't think

101

anything of it at first. I just thought it fused out, as you know they can do. Then it kept turning on and off before I heard this laugh."

The knight interrupts her with a much-needed question, "You didn't invite it in, did you?"

"No." She speaks quickly and fiercely, "I wouldn't let some demonic gate crasher into my house!"

"Fair enough," The knight calmly replies as he waves his hand to the moving quill, "It's good that you didn't and with these shadows, there is another precaution you must take."

"Which is what?" Meira sharply inquired as the knight took his time to answer.

"At this point in time you must never be alone." The knight retorts looking annoyedly at Meira with squinted eyes before he stares neutrally back at Elfina again, "This type of demon is a cowardly one and likes to keep its victims isolated before it can strike. Because of this, we'll keep a watch on your house and your store for you."

"And how will you stop it?" Elfina asks with some concern as Viola takes her hand to give her some strength.

"We are doing all that we can, Miss." He articulates to her. As the knight considers all of these beings' terrified faces, he has the feeling that these people need to have more information. However reluctant to give it, he leans closer to the group so none of the other knights can hear what he's going to say. "We think these shadow demons are being brought here by someone summoning them. We know this because these creatures are randomly attacking and killing beings of all kinds, not just a set amount of people. If they are not in control and running wild, then they have someone in this world inviting them in with some kind of dark magic. I only share this with you because I want you all to be careful."

The group for the first time is silent and unreadable. With that said, the knight walks away from them. He turns and looks towards the two knights in his line of sight. He calls out so the whole troop can hear him.

"Alright men! Outside! We have much to discuss!"

The knights from the kitchen and living room go towards the door while the two knights from the upstairs along with the psychic follow closely behind. The knight who talked to them is clearly the head knight of this troop. As the knights march outside he goes to the end of the line and follows them out.

Elfina and the rest of the group sit at that corner and watch the knights line up in her front yard as the lead knight who had talked with them gave orders. With an inaudible speech going on, the lead knight points at the knight to the far left, who gives the leader a nod in return and marches toward Elfina's stoop. He stands there with his sword unsheathed albeit ready for action if it is needed. Clearly, he is the one who is going to stay for the first night.

"Hell of a lot of help they were." Meira states sourly, breaking the silence. "I don't trust them enough to find this summoner of demons."

"What makes you say that dear?" Ozzie probes as he puts an arm around her shoulders.

"If they know all of this, they should be finding that so called summoner right now!"

"Yes, but so many people are being attacked now and they need to be protected as well." Viola says calmly, "It's obvious that they are understaffed. I don't think they have enough people to search and destroy when really all they can do is protect."

"Then I guess we will have to find this shithead enchanter ourselves." Stephan adds, "Before they attack Elfina again."

"He's right." Elfina chimes in, feeling her heart rate slow down for the first time all night, "We are going to have to do something about this ourselves. We can't just sit here and wait for something else to happen."

"You're telling me." Jacqueline agrees but the look on her face shows apprehension. "It's going to be a lot of work and fighting Elfina."

"Just a regular old party for us, isn't it?" Elfina displays resuming back to her usual cheerful self. "We can blow these guys back to hell with fireworks."

Everyone in the room laughs at last. Even with everything bad that has happened tonight they find a way to cheer themselves up.

"Seriously though guys," Ozzie pipes up as he wipes away a tear from his eye as he continues to laugh, "I do agree that Elfina shouldn't be left alone and since these guys aren't too much help, one or more of us will have to be with you all the time."

"Even when I am on the toilet?" Elfina questions him impertinently, once again causing everyone to laugh.

"How charming, Elfina," Meira cries, "But he is right. We should just stick around and keep you safe just to make sure that this shadowy fuck doesn't come back."

Elfina understands and concurs with her friends, "No, that would be good, I think. I trust you guys and know I'll be safe amongst you."

"Okay, I can stay tonight and some of tomorrow." Viola volunteers as she politely puts up her hand. "I work the later shift tomorrow at the bank."

"Sounds good." Jacqueline speaks as she stands up from the sofa. "We will take our leave now."

As they all are in agreement and after a quick sweep up of her trashed books, the rest of the clan leaves. In the antique trunk of her living room, Elfina gets out a blanket and pillow to get the sofa ready for Viola. Viola sits on her couch and watches Elfina. She can see that her friend is just exhausted now with the dark circles under her eyes and how she is having trouble keeping them open. After everything that has happened, Viola stands up and embraces Elfina after she sets everything down. She feels the nymph shudder as she knows that she is letting out a quick sob.

"Thanks for staying with me," Elfina speaks without a hint of sadness but is still not as bright as she usually is.

"No worries, Honey." Viola pats her back. "I'll let you sleep in and make you breakfast."

Elfina gives a small smile and breaks apart from Viola. "You don't have to do that."

"I want to." She says, smiling and giving Elfina's arms a friendly rub. "Go get some sleep."

Elfina gives Viola a smile and turns to leave her friend to get settled. "Sweet dreams." She calls from the staircase.

All she wants to do now is sleep and not think about demons, knights, and evil summoners of any kind. She walks back over to her bed and wraps herself up tightly in her quilt in order to gain some warmth back into her body. Tonight, she will rest and tomorrow she will figure out what has to be done.

Chapter Eight

A few days later, at her store, Elfina is sitting up on a stool behind her counter with a notebook and a pencil in her hand. She chooses not to use magic to write the notes for her because she desperately needs to do something with her hands. This can be seen by the way she spins the pencil between her fingers in one hand and taps her notebook pages with the digits in the other. She scans around the room with her eyes and can see that it isn't too busy in her store today, but she does have a good steady stream of customers. This downtime gives her some time to try and figure out who this mysterious summoner is. So far, she only has two possible people who it could be.

It could be Alistar. He is a wandering showman who keeps running into the Grim Reaper. Then there is Minerva, a hermit witch who hates having people close to her property. As Elfina reads these names in her notebook, she has to admit that even these two are very unlikely to do something like this.

Alistar is a daredevil who preforms stunts all over the realm as a means to make money. These stunts tend to be dangerous, so of course, the Grim Reaper will always be watching. Not to mention the Grim Reaper has come into her store every so often, and that doesn't make her a summoner just a merchant. Then there is Minerva; she isn't a bad woman just a little odd and anti-social. Not everyone likes having people around, but she does leave her home whenever she needs something. She is a quiet woman who only practices with herbs and the occasional crystal. Elfina can't see her summoning up demons.

She throws her pencil on the notebook and then catches a deep, annoyed breath. Running her hands through her barrette hair, Elfina couldn't shake her frustration. There are so many questions that she can't answer, and she doesn't know where to look first. Who is this stupid summoner?! Why would they do this? What could be gained by killing all of these innocent people? And her all-time favorite question:

Why her? She sits on her stool and presses her combined hands to her forehead. How could she have gotten caught up in this? How did the others get caught up in this? The victims have nothing in common and just seem like random attacks. There is not any kind of motive for any of this.

Stephan walks in from the backroom and wipes his hands on the rag that he kept in his back jeans pocket. "The wiring in the back is fixed, my dear," Stephan announces cheerfully, "Since it's my turn to babysit you, is there anything else that needs to be fixed or built?"

"No, not right now, Stephan." As Elfina looks depressingly in his direction, he knows that there is something bothering her. Although he knows, he asks her anyway, "What's wrong, Sweetheart? You're not usually this down about anything. Not crowding you, are we?"

"No, you guys could never crowd me, you know that." Elfina says, giving him a half smile, "I'm just frustrated. There are so many questions running through my head that I can't answer and don't know where to begin."

"I don't blame you for that." Stephan says as he leans over the counter facing her, "I know it's hard but there is always a place to start and I think you have found it with your own list of suspects."

He saw her notebook when he leaned over, with the names on it. She replies, "Yes but even with them I can't see them doing this. It's not in their nature or their gain to do this."

"No but at least you have that mind in motion when most others would just turn their tails in between their legs and run." Stephan says giving her a friendly pat on her arm, "That's a very strong and brave thing to do."

A little more of a smile appears on her face as she looks up at him and he continues, "Besides you have all of us to watch your back. And believe me, when we get this shit-bag, all of us will give them a taste of their own medicine."

Elfina laughs for the first time in days when she turns to him and playfully punches his shoulder. "Now I see what Jacqueline loves about you so much."

"Hey!" He yells exaggeratedly at her while returning her a frisky but tender punch on her arm.

"Oh go aw.." She begins to say but is interrupted by the bell on top of her door ringing.

In comes the familiar, funny face of Dr. Marcus Glomhammer. Elfina's face lights up the instant she sees him. Her smile widens and her teeth gleam as she eagerly stands up to greet him.

"Hi Professor! How are you these days?"

He is the extremely rare case of an actual human who could come into the Nether Realm and leave again. In the Earth Realm he is a scientist of metaphysics, mystic studies, and philosophy. A genius to say the least but according to the other humans, he is a schizophrenic. He lives oddly, inspecting the items he gets from the Nether Realm only to find that they don't seem so enchanted in other realms. He is trying to change that to give mankind a chance to experience this magical world for themselves.

"Burr burr harrumph." He always speaks when someone acknowledges him. Finally, he looks her in the eye and grins. "Elfina, I am well and you look very lovely today."

Although he speaks this with a bit of a stutter, Elfina's face brightens as she answers. "Why, thank you." She gives a bouncy curtsy to him and straightens out her long rose-colored chiffon summer dress. She walks around her counter and over to him to ask, "So what can I do for you today?"

"Burr burr, I need something that will give my mind good balance. The Dean is stressing me again." He enthusiastically spouts out. Even though she knows that this isn't true, Elfina is happy to help him out. As he walks with her, he straightens out his bow tie and runs a hand through his gray, messy, and thoroughly tangled hair. "I must look for other treasures as well while I am here."

"You always do Professor and why is that?" Elfina asks with a childlike impishness. "You have a date tonight?"

"No child no." He answers as he follows her to the tea section. Elfina giggles at that statement. If anything, she is older than him. "A man must look his best when he comes home."

It is touching to Elfina that this man considered this his home when he was born on the other side. He has such a kind old face with lovely albeit sad blue eyes that reminds her of the rain. He has a slight mustache this time and is wearing his favourite red sweater today. Elfina picks up the tea he needs and explains what it is.

"This lovely tea has mallow, mint and cardamom in it," Elfina told him as she passed him the tea. "This is a tea that is supposed to relax your mind and help it create new and fantastic ideas when the time is right."

He carefully studies the tea, turning it in all directions like if he opens it all the riches in the world will fall out of it. After he opens the tin, he puts the dry herbs to his nose and indulges in a long inhale. A dreamy haze appears in his eyes and a smile grows on his face. He looks to Elfina and nods in appreciation.

Elfina strolls over to him and with a wave of her hand, she leads Professor Glomhammer back to her counter. "Come Professor. I have a talisman that I want to show you."

Elfina kneels down behind her counter and picks up an item that is wrapped in a snow-white handkerchief. She unwraps the cloth to reveal a long oblong amethyst with the om symbol engraved across it in gold.

"It's wonderful!" The Professor gently trails his fingers across the symbol.

Elfina reaches her hand over to give it to him. "I got this talisman in the morning. It will remove all blocks and stress that comes to a person's mind."

With a very pleased and eager look, he pulls out all of the GPs in his pocket to buy both of the products. Elfina puts the talisman in a blue velvet bag and hands it to him while he puts both items into his leather satchel. Elfina knows that he will not only use both products but also study them. He can never find anything to explain why items only seem to work in the Nether Realm and nowhere else but that will never stop him. He will always keep trying to bring magic into the Earth Realm.

When he looks at Elfina, he can see that something isn't right. Her eyes are not the glittering green gems that he knows them to be.

"Are you alright my dear?" He inquires with a caring and confused look, "Is there something happening?"

Sick of pretending that something isn't happening, Elfina tells him everything about the shadow demon that had attacked her. His eyes go wide with alarm as he remembers something important that he has to share.

"I've heard some other beings talking about something like that." He pauses as if he is looking for an answer that lies deep within himself. "I've been doing some research on some similar beings and I have come up with some theories of my own."

Elfina searches his face. By the deep thorough look on his face, Elfina can tell that he has been doing a lot of work on this. He taps his index finger to his mouth as if it has the answers that he is searching for.

"What I have learned about these demons my dear is that they are usually being controlled by an intelligent manipulator," Marcus says as he begins to pace in front of her counter with his index finger still sitting lightly on his lips. He once told her that his finger usually had good ideas. Humans told him it was his illness talking, but Elfina finds it amusing.

"We know that much, Doc," Stephan tells him with slight agitation in his voice. He did not share Elfina's amusement towards the Professor. To him, this human is a little too odd.

"Well, what I am sure you don't know, my boy, is that historically speaking," Elfina raises an eyebrow at him when he calls Stephan "my boy" but chooses not to correct him. Stephan is much older than the professor too but she imagines that this poor man could not help himself. It is easy to forget where you are. Even in the Nether Realm it is possible to carry a mental illness with a person. Elfina has and will always treat every customer with compassion and understanding.

"The ones who can summon up these demons are necromancers," Marcus speaks and has both Elfina and Stephan looking astonished at him with his findings.

"Really, just them? No other kinds of black magic users?" Stephan asks as if he is expecting the unbelievable.

"Correct sir," Marcus says as he brings his shoulder bag forward. "Black magic can call up all kinds of demons but when someone uses the dead for power, these are the particular demons that like to pop up and maybe even give the practitioner the illusion of getting what they are looking for out of it. I hope this helps you out some. Good day!"

After taking all of his purchases, Marcus leaves the shop quickly. The two of them still look wide-eyed at the door with their mouths slightly hanging open. The two of them are stunned. Suddenly it all makes sense to them now. Demons are just suddenly popping up with no apparent motive and they need to be invited into someone's home or strike out in the open away from anyone who can easily intervene. Always hiding in the shadows and that is what a necromancer does as well. Elfina knows that they could never actually face anyone living which is why they prefer the dead. Call it cowardice or a complex but that is what a necromancer thinks.

"We've got to tell the rest." Elfina puts a demanding hand on Stephan's arm.

"No, we should tell the proper authorities that is what we should do." Stephan counters.

"They haven't done anything but sweep through my house and keep a constant watch on me." Elfina connects, "Besides these damn demons are keeping them way too busy. I read today that even the training warriors and amazons are out there chasing them."

With a reluctant look on his face, Stephan nods. He knows what has to be done. "We are on our own. We have to talk to the rest and then I think we should go see Javas."

"You're right. He might know something." Elfina agrees, "I think we will be able to handle this, Stephan. We just need a plan."

He chuckles at her, amused by her easy personality, "Oh and do you have this master plan?"

She raises an eyebrow, and shoots him a teasing look, "No, I think I will. I leave that up to you."

*****

That evening, they all agreed to go visit Javas. With Viola looking into his fish tank, silently communicating with them via the aquatic telepathy that all sea creatures share, Jacqueline and Voltaire stare at each other with mutual dislike, and Meira along with Osmond, are scrolling through a pile of Javas' magical books. Elfina is standing next to Javas, looking into his looking glass with him, only to find nothing.

"Damn!" Elfina slowly shakes her head. "It's just too difficult to see anything."

"Patience my dear." Javas puts a calm hand on her arm, "It takes time and together we always find something."

"I know it's just not like this for me. I only get a vision when I get one. It always comes on its own."

Javas nods his head as he can see that she is having a hard time with this. "Why don't you go to the ice box and fix us all something to eat? You are a bundle of energy right now, and it might do you some good to cook."

Elfina has to agree with that statement. Getting some food for everyone might be a little more calming than looking into that gigantic mirror. Her own frustration could be blocking her. Opening the refrigerator, Elfina finds apples, bread, and enough vegetables to make a salad. Unfortunately for Jacqueline, she would have to make do with a little clam and tomato juice.

"Feeling like dieting again, Jacqueline?" Elfina asks her friend as she pulls out the tomato and clam juice. In response, Jacqueline shrugs her shoulders and scowls back at the owl. Jacqueline has nothing against Javas but she really hates his bird and his house. His hut is too dilapidated by vampire standards and she can not stand things that are dirty and messy. That's the same reason why she hates his bird. Voltaire always squawks at her as if to insult her. *Birds*, Jacqueline has always hated them. In her opinion, they are better off being blood-drained and perhaps eaten rather than kept as pets.

As Elfina manages to toss up a salad for everyone, Stephan bursts into the house in his wolf form. Jacqueline is relieved to stop looking at that impertinent feathered freak and gives her husband a half-smile at his arrival.

"You're late." She tells him slyly as he begins his transformation back into a man.

"Sorry, Babe." He says as he walks over to her to give her a quick and sweet kiss on the mouth. "But those guys are having a hard time finding any time to listen to me with all these shadows running around."

Viola turns from the tank and looks over to Stephan. "Are they going to do anything about it?"

"No, not right now." He retorts as he gazes over to her. "These guys really are so tied up with the demons that finding the source seems so impossible now."

"So, it is up to us then," Meira speaks out as she puts the book back on the pile beside her. She straightens out her dirty white tank shirt to take a quick, calming breath.

Stephan nods towards her and puts an arm around his wife's shoulders as she hisses over at Voltaire. Meira looks over to Ozzie and rolls her eyes. While rubbing her sweaty palms on her tight brown pants, Meira walks over to Elfina. Ozzie loves seeing his girlfriend in those tight pants and cute tops. It is always erotic to see her hair tied back in that leather thong she is wearing right now. Meira could always pull off the tomboyish look and make it super sexy as he trails his eyes on her long, athletic body. Then there is the scent of gardenia flowing from her body that drives him crazy. As if sensing his thoughts, Meira casts a look over in his direction and winks at him.

"Tonight, you are mine." Her eyes say to him.

"I knew we were going to have to do this ourselves," Meira speaks as she looks from Ozzie to everyone else with a serious face. "But we need to know our next step."

"Yes, and make sure it's the right one." Viola says showing a fearful but determined look on her face. "We can't just rush into something dangerous without being prepared for it."

Suddenly Javas announces loudly with his eyes wide and mouth wide open, "I see something now!"

Everyone rushes over to him, and Elfina holds onto his arm as she can see it too. It is the outside of Lady Merida's mansion. At first, they see the outside of the mansion itself at a distance. It looks uninhabited with its normally glistening stones covered in soot, the garden unkempt, and the windows no longer transparent but mucked up with grime. Then the inside of the mansion appears in the ballroom.

Again, nothing is there but empty spaces and dirty floors. A small grey feather floats through the room yet there is no sign of any life in there.

It didn't make sense that anything would still be there but something tells Elfina that there is a clue hidden in there. The others can't see because they don't have the gift of sight that both Elfina and Javas have.

"Guys!" She shouts out loud and the group gathers around her. "I know what we have to do." She recounts seeing Lady Merida's mansion and how it looks. "We have to go there and fast!"

Elfina searches all of her friends' faces and tries eagerly to read what they are thinking, even though telepathy is not her forte. She can at least tell that Jacqueline and Viola think that it might be a good idea considering they have raised their eyebrows, slight nods on their unsmiling chins, and they rotate their eyes to look at each other. Meira on the other hand, clearly thinks that it is not the best idea with her eyebrows lifted, mouth open, and her complexion beginning to pale.

"Are you sure we should go Elfina?" Meira questions with a somewhat cynical rise of her left eyebrow. "I mean the authorities have all been there and found nothing. What possible chance do we have?"

"Maybe we can find something." Viola jumps in, "I mean not all psychics can pick up things. Just the one that is meant to find the answer and Elfina might be the one to find something."

"Hmm." Meira taps her chin thoughtfully, "Good point."

"Besides the investigation is finished over there so it only makes sense that we can go there now," Jacqueline tells her.

"Yeah." Elfina lightheartedly continues, "Breaking and entering an angel's home, facing a necromancer, and imminent danger. What are we waiting for?"

Everyone looks at her and with all of them smiling at her, they nod in agreement.

"This is the best lead we have, and who knows? Maybe we can catch a lucky break." Elfina puts in.

"Right!" Meira pulls her fist down like a great big yes! "We will go to Lady Merida's mansion first thing in the morning and find out what is happening."

Javas looks at them and gives them a gentle reminder. "Well, in an angel's house (even if they are no longer present), there is no better place to catch a miracle."

"We better head home and prepare," Jacqueline says as she turns to face her husband.

"I can't go with you," Stephan declares looking first to his wife and then the rest of the group. "Remember I have to fix the sink that you came through, Elfina."

"Yeah." Ozzie looks to Elfina with an impish gleam in his eyes. "I think you might have burst a pipe when you came through it that day."

"Sorry," Elfina says sweetly pouting at him while matching his naughty look with her own.

"No worries, Love. I'm just glad that you are okay." Ozzie smiles over at her. "By the way, I will be there to supervise. Will you four be alright, going yourselves?"

"Absolutely." Jacqueline purrs and turns her attention to Elfina. "Who is staying with you tonight, Elfina?"

"Viola." Elfina answers while putting her arm around her shoulders. "She is the only one who can get me up early in the morning. It's kind of annoying."

With that the six of them walk out of Javas' hut and go their separate ways. Elfina and Viola walk together towards Mystina Forest. It is going to be hard for Elfina to get up so early in the morning when all she wants to do is sleep in. But just this once, she knows she can't do that now. On that day when all of this is over, Elfina plans on taking a day off just so she can spend it sleeping. Somehow, she has a good feeling that it will be happening soon.

Chapter Nine

Bright and early that morning, Jacqueline, Elfina, Meira, and Viola walk into Lady Merida's mansion. It is still so beautiful and warm there. The exorcists must have gone through that place already and made the vibes good again. That is an extremely difficult feat to do when it comes to the fact that an angel had died there. All the women saw the angel and her stoned self on the stage in the ballroom, looking peaceful and ethereal. The four of them start to feel the tears form in their eyes. It is so nice not to see her look so anguished and tortured like she was at the funeral. Each woman secretly scolds themselves in their own silent ways, knowing that they are there for a purpose. The ladies form a circle facing each other.

"Okay let's look around. We are bound to find something here." Meira pipes up as she gazes around the ballroom. "I'll take a look around the balconies."

"I'll see what I can find in around the east wing down here," Viola states and looks towards Jacqueline.

"I'll look around the entryway," Jacqueline announces in the circle of women, and Elfina reveals.

"I'll check the ballroom and around the stage. Perhaps it's here where we will find some answers."

With a nod from all of them, the women part ways and begin to look around in places that they had assigned themselves to. Elfina inspects the room, trying to find anything in the open, empty space of the ballroom. She is more than sure that she could find any kind of clue that might be hidden around there. Seeing the empty bar close to the west wing, she has an idea that it might be the best place to start searching if anything was missed.

A wickedly amused expression forms on her face. She thinks it would be an added bonus if she manages to find any unlikely alcohol around. Pacing over to the bar she starts to contemplate everything that she is looking at to find anything worth investigating. It seems like nothing is there but soon she hears what sounds like a soft rustling of feathered wings. Her gaze lands on Lady Merida's statue. She sees a piece of paper floating from behind the statue to the ground in front of the stage.

Elfina walks over and picks up the paper only to find that there is nothing on it. Confused, she continues to study it until she finds herself having a vision.

Everything is dark, and she can not see anything but in mere seconds she sees a symbol. It is something so familiar that she tries to look at it closer. However, she can not remember where she saw it last and what it means. It looks like an upside-down V with a small circle above the tip of it. After she comes out of the vision, Elfina catches her breath and looks around to make sure she is back in the ballroom. Luckily, she is.

"Hey, ladies! I found something." She calls out to all of her friends.

As quickly as they can they arrive by her side, and Elfina tells them what she saw in her vision. Viola quickly takes the piece of paper that Elfina is holding out to show them. She brings it close to her face and gently sniffs it.

"This isn't ordinary paper Elfina. This is parchment." Viola says, looking at it closely.

"So?" Elfina questions and maintains, "There's lots of parchment paper around."

"Not like this. This is very ancient and could be worth a fortune on this small piece alone."

"What about this symbol?" Meira enquires as she glances towards Elfina, "What does it look like?"

After her questions, Elfina took out a notepad and pen from her purse to draw what she had seen. After finishing the drawing, Elfina holds it out to them and Meira is the first one to take it. The others scan the drawing on the notepad and look perplexingly at it. Elfina can tell by the somewhat irritated look on their faces that it too is familiar but none of them could remember where they saw it.

"What is it an arrow?" Viola scrunches up her face to concentrate on what she is seeing, "An A?"

"Who knows? We'll have to look it up," Jacqueline shakes her head.

"It is so familiar to me." Meira puts out to her friends. "Tell you guys what. I will take this home and look it up. I have a whole lighting tech on symbols and I am sure I can find it there."

"Thank the universe for outer space technology." Elfina sighs stirring her head with a relieved look on her face.

"I know I can't believe the other worlds don't have it," Viola adds with a proud gleam in her eye.

"I wonder why that is?" Elfina smugly says.

"Probably because they haven't discovered it yet or they want to make their lives a little too complicated." Jacqueline sarcastically hypothesizes to her friends, "Alright Osmond is watching out for you tonight, Viola is seeing you tomorrow, and I am with you the next day after. Correct?"

"Works for me." Elfina casually shrugs her shoulders.

"Good." Meira nods. "It'll take some time for me to find this symbol but I promise as soon as I find it, I will bring it to you guys."

Bowing their heads in agreement, they all leave the manor through the front door. Elfina is happy to not only have some kind of step forward but humor back into her life. Then again, she knows she is never without it. That in itself is a small miracle.

120

That day at Elfina's store is a colourful one. She has had many customers in the morning and early afternoon. She thanks the almighty that she has Jacqueline with her today. Right now, she is putting away her glass jars full of herbs on the shelves. Jacqueline is always a good worker but Elfina knows that this isn't Jacqueline's scene at all. All she wants is to paint and be social which is her vampire friend's special gift. So, she understands why Jacqueline won't normally work here unless she had to. Besides, Elfina loves that the store is just hers and hers alone. Now that the late afternoon is upon them, Elfina watches as three dragon riders from three old countries come into her store as soon as she strolls out of the back room.

"Ah! My lady, Elfina I am glad your shop is open today." Greets the Indian dragon rider. "I am in serious need of your help."

She walks over to the counter and looks over to him smiling her biggest smile, "How can I help you today, Haroun?"

"It's my Asheem." Elfina knows that he is talking about his dragon. A ruby-skinned Arabic Wyvern that always seems to bother him at some point or other. He is a dragon of will and spirit. She finds Asheem to be a more admirable creature than any other that she has ever known. But with much amusement to many, the dragon doesn't seem to respect poor Haroun at all. "He keeps spouting these insults at me. That silly creature listens to my wife more than me."

As Elfina listens to Haroun's complaints, she remembers what it was that Javas told her about dragons. They may look like large lizards that breath fire, ice, or even lightning but deep down they have the behavior of both dogs and parrots. They can be tamed and able to do one's bidding but they can talk like the earth's realm's most revered birds. They love to mimic words and continue to do so over and over again until you are ready to pull your hair out.

Elfina takes a look over at Jacqueline who has a fixed bored look on her face until she raises an eyebrow at Elfina. She is wondering how her fey friend is going to fix this one. It's always so much fun to see what her unpredictable nymph friend is going to do to solve the puzzle.

"Haroun, the dragon is an animal just like any other." She says to her heavily cloaked customer. "He just needs patience, kindness and persistence."

"Yes, I know my dear." He utters to her with an almost humorous but desperate look. "But he still won't stop and I need some items that are said to help me with this kind of problem."

When the young English dragon rider goes outside everyone hears a deep, booming voice speak from outside the shop. "Your mother has the face of a toilet…"

The door closes before the dragon finishes his insult, leaving everyone in the store aghast at what the dragon has said. Hearing what is going on out there, Elfina knows exactly what he needs. She walks over towards the shelf, she picks up a small drum with two strings, and a bead on each of the sides with a small handle.

Elfina explains as she gives him the drum. "This drum will not only call your dragon to you but it will calm any anxiety that he has. And that dragon seems to have a lot of it."

"Thank you Elfina," Haroun says animatedly, putting his hands together and bows.

"Don't thank me yet." Elfina light-heartedly tells, looking at the great red jewel that he has on his turban, she notices that it isn't glowing the way a dragon stone should. "When was the last time you charged your stone Haroun?"

"That would be…" As he pauses to think about it, Elfina can tell he has not done it in a while.

"I see." Elfina suddenly speaks. "Well, that's why he's listening to your wife and not you."

She holds out her hand. With a sigh, he takes the stone off his head and gives it to her. He is resigned and that in itself is a problem. He shakes his head and realizes that his wife is right in saying that forgetfulness gets him into trouble.

As she walks into the back room, Elfina turns on this small stone outdoor fire chimenea-like machine called a universe energy machine or UEM. Small orbs start to fill the room while the machine makes almost an aurora borealis wave over the whole room. Elfina watches the orbs move towards the dragon stone as they surround the gem to fill it with a bright light. As the jewel shines, it becomes alive again. Since it is finished, Elfina takes it back to Hauroon in her store immediately.

"Oh yes of course." Haroun says as he hands her five pouches of dragon dust. "Thank you again, Elfina. Your grace and kindness will bring good fortune to you. This I know to be true."

As Elfina smiles at him, Jacqueline looks out the door at the strange noise and says, "Jiao-Long." She announces to the Chinese dragon rider, looking over to her from the wall of figurines, "Your dragon is female right?"

"Yes." He replies.

"Is she in heat?" Jacqueline asks, trying to smother a laugh.

"No, she shouldn't be for a couple of days. Why?" He feels the curiosity rise in him as she inquires with these strange questions.

"Haroun's dragon is having a little fun with your dragon." Jacqueline chuckles.

"What?!" Jiao-Long yells as he runs from the shelves to the door. "Haroun!"

Haroun too runs to the door, muttering something in his native tongue then yells at his dragon. After the riders dash out the door, Elfina looks out the window beside Jacqueline to see that the red dragon is on top of the blue dragon. The two of them, watch the three men try and get Asheem off of Chun, and erupt with laughter. So did the pedestrians out on the street. When they finally got Asheem off of Chun with a dragon handler. A dragon handler is a large lasso-like staff that is surrounded by a special metal called Brosium. It lights up as soon as it touches a dragon's neck and helps the riders get their dragons under control.

Asheem the red dragon bellows as soon as he is off Chun the blue dragon. "Haroun's an idiot!"

This has both Elfina and Jacqueline laughing so hard that they almost fall on the floor.

"My god Elfina." Jacqueline wipes away a tear from her misty grey eyes, "I didn't understand why you liked owning a store so much but now I see you get some pretty intense if not interesting people in here."

"That's nothing." Elfina says as she walks back towards her desk with Jacqueline following closely behind her. "Once, there was this mime that came into my store."

When both women sit at the counter, Elfina takes her into a story about a troll trying to pretend he was a mime. Trolls are very short in stature but taller than dwarves or leprechauns. They are also a lot wider. They often have skin that is so wrinkled and dry that they look almost like shrunken heads.

*****

This troll's name was Nick and he was studying to be a mime albeit he was not a very good one. One day he came into Elfina's shop and was looking for someone to fix his gas problem. But he was not supposed to tell her that of course. Instead, he acted it out with all kinds of gestures and movements that his short arms and legs could not hold out.

As Elfina watched this poor, unfortunate soul in black and white face make-up, she couldn't understand what he was trying to say. He kept waving his arms in the air like he was trying to imitate a snake.

Elfina furrowed her face at him and shook her head while shrugging her shoulders.

"I'm not following you, Nick."

Suddenly, he put his big hand on his stomach and the other on his mouth. Elfina contemplated walking to him just to shake him and say, "use your words!" She takes a step forward to him but stops as soon as this poor troll's discomfort becomes more than apparent. He let out a huge FART that rocked the whole store. Elfina scrambled towards her figurine wall to keep them from falling off the shelf.

The noxious smell invaded her shop, and she had a hard time trying to stay conscious of the way she had to stagger around her store. After opening all the windows and doors to get rid of the smell, Elfina goes to her herbal shelf behind the counter to give him the ingredients he needs. She gave him a mixture of ginger root, crushed green cardamom seeds, and a small vial of lime juice. She passed the ingredients to him from behind her counter.

"Now, Nick, mix these together and drink it down fast," Elfina instructs holding a silk handkerchief over her mouth and nose. "You should feel better in no time."

With that he thanked her (in mime) and left.

*****

"So, what happened to him after that?" Jacqueline asks leaning in on the counter.

"He decided that he was better off to be a clown." Elfina says with a big grin, "Now he does magic tricks and uses his farts as his acts."

As they both laugh, Elfina points out. "Well, he is very successful now in this world and the next. The only thing that's wrong with this scenario is that he has to get his skin temporarily stretched when he has to go into the Earth Realm."

"Does he still come here?"

"He does." Elfina answers leaning up against her counter. "He keeps coming back for the gas mixture and for the cream that keeps the stretches in his face last for a little longer. It works."

The bell on her door rings as Meira runs in with a big sheet of paper in her hand.

"Girls, I have found it!" Meira's eyes are alight with excitement.

"The symbol?" Elfina stands up with an air of liberation on her face. "What is it?"

Meira gives her friends the sheet of paper. Elfina and Jacqueline check closely at the symbol and its description. It is the symbol of the Scientific Institute of Atlantis. This is where the best minds of the Nether Realm study everything from magic to technology, from nature to the future. It is not a surprise to them that someone from that academy is behind all this. Not that it is corrupt. Quite the contrary. They have strict rules there that any practice of the evil arts will have them not only expelled from the premises but persecuted to the fullest extent of the law. They do talk about the subject as they look at all points of the magical spectrum and sometimes that can be dark.

"That's why it was so familiar." Elfina says looking at both of her girlfriends. "We saw that symbol when we went to Atlantis for that vacation fifty years ago. How could we have forgotten?"

"It was a while since we went on vacation." Jacqueline supposes as she shakes her head. "It's not surprising that we forgot that. It was just a small thing really, that we saw and I am pretty sure that it was only once."

"It's the best scientific study of our world." Meira points out. "We would have remembered seeing this symbol too. There must have been some special reason why we all forgot it."

"Look, that is not the point here." Elfina chimes into both of them. "Let it go girls. We found out what the symbol is. Now we have to find out if there was a necromancer there."

Both Jacqueline and Meira see that she is right. However, they absolutely hate that she is. The uneasiness that they feel about this situation has the two of them look to each other with concern. Meira feels her stomach turn at just the thought of how dangerous this is going to be. While Jacqueline feels her undead blood stop cold in her veins due to the uncertainty of this situation.

"We better call Viola and our men," Jacqueline announces uneasily. "We clearly have a lot to discuss."

Both she and Meira turn to find the crystal ball to make some calls. Now that their next step is established Elfina ponders to herself about the next one. The next step is finding out about this necromancer who has ties with this institute. She just hopes to find the answer before it is too late.

Chapter Ten

After taking the day off, Elfina decides to go to the Scarlars University library to look up anything she can find about necromancy in Atlantis. She is sitting at a long wooden table in an equally wooden chair, going through book after book and newspaper after newspaper. Elfina just can not find anything about that subject in any source she is looking into.

Frustrated, she thumps the book down on the rest of the books that she has already looked at. She shakes her head, pulls her fingers through her hair, and stares around the library to give her tired eyes a break.

This place is an endless maze of books, scrolls, and other tools of knowledge. Whatever a being is looking for, they would most definitely find it here despite Elfina's current hardship already. The library itself is a round room that has two long stories of shelves that have anything and everything that would keep information on all esoteric topics. Things like occult trends, urban legends, ancient fairy folklore, and the whole works can be found here.

Her eyes trailed up to the ceiling, which is a dome of clear stained-glass windows in a vine-like design that would sporadically change whenever it wanted to. For some reason, no one ever finds it distracting but calming instead. At least, Elfina finds it calming. Her theory is that due to some kind of enchantment, it has a tranquil effect on the library patrons that eases their minds and helps them focus.

The center of the library has tables where everybody has a place to sit and read with the added convenience of their own self-flamed lantern. A rustic round metal lantern that has a solar flame that lights up automatically. For if dusk creeps in on them, a magic flame would appear in it. This makes reading so much easier at night.

Elfina checks behind her at the little kiosk that is selling coffee, tea, and treats. As she is feeling so unbelievably drained, she stands up from her chair to do something about that. At that point, she chooses to go for one of those delicious chocolate tarts.

Elfina sighed as she walked over to the golden-red-skinned, three-eyed Devi named Durga. An Indian goddess of protection, motherhood, strength, and war. With her ten arms and hands, she is serving up everyone their hot beverages and snacks with speedy efficiency. Her presence alone is a wonderful protective feature of the library, which is why you'll never find a demon in here.

"Back again Durga?" Elfina asks the Hindu goddess while blinking her eyes and trying desperately to keep them open.

"Oh yeah. Everyone needs some nurturing and humor around here. This place can be a little too quiet sometimes." Elfina nods, admiring Durga's energy and vitality. Nothing seems to tire her out. "You look like you need it more than anyone else here today, my young nymph. A gold piece for your thoughts?"

"No, it's just tiring." Elfina leans forward and puts her sleepy face against the palm of her hand. "Okay, I will take the chocolate tart please and I'll have another cup of your jasmine green tea."

"Very good my dear." Reaching one arm to the canister, Durga is fixing up a teacup with another while brushing her long beautiful black hair aside. She senses turmoil when she looks at Elfina with her center eye. This is the eye that can see things that others can't. "Are you sure you don't want to talk about it?"

Elfina shakes her head at Durga. "I wish I could, but I have a lot of ground to cover. Thanks anyway Durga."

She pays her tab and takes her treat back to the table she is working at. Elfina takes her small fork to cut it into her rich, decadent pastry. When she brings the contents to her lips, she closes her eyes in ecstasy as the rich, velvety taste reinvigorates her. After she leans down towards the sweet-smelling contents of her teacup, Elfina thinks of how she can make all of this strenuous research easier for herself. Clearly, all these books are not helping as she skims her eyes over to them again.

Behind this circular room are more shelves of books, scrolls, and tablets, but there is also a room of information beams. Information beams are simple-looking crystal balls that the star clans have given to the mystics over millennia ago. They are super simple to use and have been a blessing to scholars all over the realm. As soon as a being asks the crystal ball what they are looking for these beams of light come out from inside of them. For anything that a person wants to know, these lights show off the answers to the question. It is similar to that of a film, video, or picture show.

Elfina thinks that it might be a good idea to look at them even if they are expensive and always busy. After finishing her dessert, Elfina stands up from her table to walk over to the beam room. She sees to her surprise that there aren't very many people in there. Happy about this situation a small relieved smile creeps on across her face.

With a spring in her step, she decides to have a go at the information beams as she walks inside the dark room. The only light she can see is that of the crystal balls that other beings are using and the small lights in the ceiling resembling stars in a dark sky. Thank you to the star clans!

Elfina is not worried about getting spied on because other beings would not see what she is going to look up, just as she can't see what they are doing. The library put a privacy spell on each crystal ball, which keeps others from plagiarizing others' work and keeps research sources anonymous. The library has always had a strict privacy policy that is not meant to interfere with a person's life. Another reason why these techno-beams are so expensive. After putting her 1,500 gold pieces into the slot, Elfina speaks into the microphone, "Tell me about the necromancer in the Scientific Institute of Atlantis, please."

With that, the crystal ball begins to light up with an array of different colors and a V-shaped light appears reaching up to the ceiling. It shows a man with black disheveled hair. He is standing in a courtroom before the juridical council of Atlantis. This consists of twelve members dressed in black robes and white rolled wigs. They stand before him on a large podium looking down on him. With this man's angry, glaring eyes and thin lips twitching in a snarl, he begins to scream at them.

"I am a scientist! I am doing some intensive work to help Atlantis achieve great power! If you stop me now, all will be lost!" After that, he does nothing but shout out a bunch of gibberish that no one could possibly understand. When he starts flailing his arms and legs like a toddler throwing a tantrum, the guards have to grab him. After a long struggle, the guards manage to restrain him by pinning him down to the ground. However, the professor still keeps on shaking his head and yelling out cuss words.

"Well done, Genius." Elfina speaks sardonically out loud to the screen. "Not such a smart man now, are you?"

The beam changes and it shows off a newspaper article with this crazed man's picture on it. He looks less disheveled and a lot colder. His light blue eyes look completely devoid of emotion and soulless albeit filled with logic and intelligence. It makes her shiver just a bit and yet grateful that he was never her teacher. His name is Atrium Enzor, and he used to teach the history of dark magic at the SIA.

The article reads. "Disgraced professor at the academy apprehended for abusing corpses from the Earth Realm. Atrium Enzor used dead bodies, carving symbols, and necrophilia for practicing the dark arts as a means to boost Atlantis' hold and control on the dark realm."

Practicing the dark craft in the Nether Realm for any reason is illegal, and people are often sentenced to life imprisonment or worse. They can get sent to the dark world for such crimes. Elfina looks at this name again, "Atrium Enzor" and writes it down on her notepad. She skims down the article further and reads this,

"Atrium Enzor Escaped! Whereabouts unknown."

"Gotcha." Elfina cheers to herself as she now knows who this culprit could be.

This man used to be on the island of Atlantis, which is why she had that vision back at Lady Merida's mansion. She also feels relieved to have found a suspect who has the skill and motive to do all of this injustice to so many people. As she walks out of the beam room, Elfina flips through her notepad and scans the information that she has acquired. She closes her book and has a thought.

Perhaps she should take this information to the authorities. With a single nod of her head, this sounds like a good idea to her but at the same time it is getting dark. Elfina looks up to the ceiling window to see how true that is and decides that she should probably leave. She knows that this information would be useful to the Knights and Valkyries but It's hard to be safe with a bunch of shadows running around. On top of that, she did promise her friends that she would go straight to Meira's after spending time at the library investigating alone. It will just have to wait until the morning.

*****

Elfina feels a cold wind brush against her while she walks along the village sidewalk. She knows that this is not a normal current of air that she is used to but something much darker. This is a sign that she has to call Henry to come get her and take her away. After all, her sweet ghostly friend would always say that he and his carriage were at her service. Besides, with how dark it's getting and with the shadow demons keeping the Knights and Valkyries busy, Elfina knows even more so now that going to Meira's by carriage is the best way to go.

Elfina closes her eyes, puts her fingertips to her temples, and concentrates on making an important telepathic call. Before she could call upon the telepathic operators with her mind, she felt a small fist tug at her skirt. Looking down, she sees a little ghost boy holding her skirt trying to get her attention. He is about 4'5 with light-colored hair, pale blue eyes, and transparent pale skin to match. On his little face he wears an expression of sadness.

Studying each other for a few seconds, Elfina kneels at his eye level and expresses, "What's wrong? Did something happen?"

"I know who you are looking for." He chimes in a wistful whisper.

Elfina can not hide her curiosity as she gazes at the boy with a raised eyebrow. She does not know how this small child could know who she is and who she is looking for. Especially when the authorities don't even know who had put this plague on the world, "What do you mean?"

"The evil one who made these shadows that are hurting everyone."

The boy stares in the other direction as Elfina stands back up to look at whatever this apparition is looking at. Then with his dark-circled eyes looking back up at her, he tugs on her skirt again, pointing a tiny finger in the direction she is peering at. Together the two of them start walking in that direction. He removes his hand as he leads her down the street with dusk approaching them both.

As they continue to walk, Elfina looks up at all the houses and sees that the people in them are peeking out but hiding away as soon as they see someone observing back at them. It is very odd and Elfina wonders if this town is at the core of all the shadow attacks.

Before she knows it, Elfina finds herself just outside of the village. The ice-cold fear trembles up her spine as she stops to glance ahead. It is too overwhelming. The feeling that the darkness is going to swallow her whole like a giant whale against a small guppy keeps entering her mind. How can she press forward when she has never faced anything like this? Not to mention, that next to this little ghost boy looking up into her face right now, she is alone.

"It's this way." The boy announces still holding her hand.

"I'm afraid," Elfina tells him simply and plainly.

"So are they." He points to the Knight and Valkyrie Station on the other side of the road. Elfina looks back down at the boy and knows she must do the hardest thing that she is ever going to do. She takes a deep breath in, and she presses on with the small boy.

Everything around her seems so dead. The trees look like they were charred black and lifeless like they have been burned beyond any recovery. She can not even see the grass on her sandaled feet, but she feels the wet cold slime of them on her toes as she continues to walk. And then there is the sky. It seems to have a black cloud above it to block out any light. If she has any hope of finding her way home, it will have vanished into the heavy, oppressive air that is all around her.

A few steps more is when she sees it. A tall, dilapidated mansion with a tower that has a large round window that looks almost like an angry eyeball trying to find its worst enemy. Everything is off its hinges, with holes in various parts of this mansion, and the front porch has several rotting plants growing through the boards. This place gives her the creeps. So much so that she places a hand on her queasy stomach, hoping she will not throw up.

With a small nudge on her hip, she looks down at the little boy as he points to the house. He whispers into her ear, "The bad man is in there. He is always in there."

Suddenly a strange light briefly explodes out of the tower and several shadows start to come out of all the cracks and holes of the house. The little boy then yanks her hand and runs with her until they find a bush to hide in.

"This is the place where he is hiding?" Elfina whispers to the small boy as she watches all the shadows flying in random directions.

"Yeah." The boy whispers back and looks at her, "I found this place after I talked to the knight guys about what I saw."

Looking back at the sad-faced ghost, Elfina studies his face and asks, "What did you see?"

"I saw them suck the life out of the vampire that keeps walking around the village at night."

"Nico." Elfina murmurs, shaking her head. She knows that she can not grieve for him now. "How did you find this place?"

"That shadow guy was still around so I followed him here." He whispers to her, and it startles her what a foolish thing this small boy did. Dead or not.

"That was a very brave thing to do, but never ever do that again. It is dangerous!"

"I'm dead though." He whines.

Sympathy comes first to Elfina before the empathy of a small boy who wants to do the right thing and help. She cannot think to ill of him, especially since she is the exact same way as she is going to face the beast head-on soon enough. "Maybe but they still might find a way to hurt you, kiddo. Now did you tell the authorities this?"

"Yeah, but they can't see it." He tells her. "It's like all of them are blind or something."

Elfina now understands why no one could find this man. It is plain and simple. The necromancer is using cloaking and glamour spells to block himself from anyone be it gods, guardians, and public authorities who could do something to stop him. Just by doing this he sends them on a wild goose chase. This is truly despicable. It is clear to her now that she is the only one who can do something about this.

She decides that for now she has to leave and prepare herself for a nasty war with this maniac.

"Okay." Elfina kneels, takes the little boy's hand again, and looks him straight in the eye. "You can't ever come back here again but I promise you that this nightmare will be over soon."

With that, both the ghost and nymph make their way back from where they came. In her mind, Elfina begins to formulate a plan. The first thing she plans to do is tell Javas and the rest of her friends what she has found out. She truly believes that this all is going to end soon but, in the meantime, she must do what scares her to death. Luckily, she is not without determination. She walks back in the opposite direction with the ghost, mentally preparing herself for the battle ahead.

*****

Down in the underwater city of Aquamarine, Viola goes through her usual cash-out routine behind the front desk. A big yawn escapes her mouth, and she daintily covers it with her hand. She is happy that the day is almost over as she looks up at the clock above the door.

Not as happy as she and the rest of the employees will be tomorrow. Everybody is looking forward to their paycheques coming the next day. Also, she has a feeling that she is going to get that promotion to the bank manager position. This is why she promised that she would lock up for the night.

So, here she is in front of the cashier's desk for a little while longer and does her duties there instead of going to the coffee room to kick back and kill time. It is important to stay here just in case there is a last-minute walk-in customer. Nevertheless, she made a deal to herself earlier that she would close as soon as she finished everything that her boss had told her to do.

Accidentally, Viola knocks down the brochures off the desk with her hand as she turns in her stool. With a weary sigh, she swoops down to pick them up as she hears the welcome bell ring at the door.

"Hello. Welcome to the Nether Realm International Bank. I will be with you in a moment." She says just as she scoops up the brochures and neatly places them in a pile. With a last-minute customer like this, her day is indeed very profitable. The higher office is going to see this for sure which makes her smile at the thought.

She plops herself back up on the stool, puts the brochures back into their slot, and looks past her glass window to properly greet her customer. She does not see anyone in front of the counter as she should. Confusion hits her first as she squints her eyes at this unusual sight past the window. She knows it is not a ghost or a poltergeist because she can always detect them.

Her intuition tells her that she must look up, and what she sees nearly frightens her to death. A dark cloud-like mist is above her head, with its razor teeth materialising in the center of it. In the nick of time, Viola nimbly swims over the glass on the desk and dashes out the door when it drops down from the ceiling.

She looks through the glass door to see to see this thing watching her with its menacing red eyes and lipless mouth. It hovers midwater behind her desk, not moving or blinking. Thinking fast she locks the front door, hoping that the shadow is still inside and stays in there. Now, she is in trouble and does not know how she can get herself out of it. She instantly decides to go to the Knights and Valkyries.

When the demon suddenly appears before her, it tries to grab her with its long shadowy tentacle. Viola swiftly swims up and prevents its arm from coming around her. It looks up at her and flashes its teeth with annoyance. Its bright red eyes flicker as Viola begins to swim away as fast as she can. Instead of feeling its initial annoyance the demon starts to laugh. It clearly has found another lovely little challenge and it is going to enjoy trying to catch this one. Now the chase begins.

Chapter Eleven

Viola knows that this thing is coming after her. The cold feeling of it getting closer and closer keeps creeping into her mind. Against her usual good judgement, she swims out of the city and keeps on going until she sees the old sunken ship ahead of her.

Everyone in Aquamarine knows that this was John Cabot's old boat that sank when he accidentally hit a portal in 1499. He was going through the Northwest Passage when he was trying to get to Asia from Italy for a spice trade. Poor guy didn't realize his trip would lead him to another realm and the god Zues was having another quarrel with his wife, Hera. His ship got caught in the middle and is now rubble under the sea.

John Cabot and his crew are fine though. Some chose to go back to the Earth Realm via reincarnation while others have settled somewhere in the realm. But that is a story for another time.

Viola uses this chance to hide in the sunken ship's cabin. She knows that she should be at the Knights and Valkyries right now. But the truth is this creature keeps blocking her way and her only reaction is to run away. As soon as she can escape, she will go to the authorities. The shadow does not seem to see her as it flows from porthole to porthole: Slowly slithering as if it is an eel hunting for its next meal.

"It does not see me." Viola thinks to herself as she allows herself to have a deep, alleviated breath out.

Only relief takes her over as she now feels safe. She closes her eyes and slinks down to the broken floorboards. She presses her forehead to her folded arms that are resting on her bent tail. Her heart rate starts to lower and she decides that it is time to make a telepathic call to the Knights and Valkyries.

As soon as she opens her eyes and looks up to the ceiling, she tenses again as she spots the shadow coming through the cracks just overhead. With its teeth snarling down at her and its illuminating red eyes glaring at her, it charges at her again. Luckily, with her great agility she swims in a flip to the opposite end of the cabin.

When she hits herself against the corner, she stares at her attacker. The mist around this shadow starts to form into the shape of a man. This man seems to have a fedora hat on and a long black trench coat but no other defining features that a person can point out.

"You will not get away." It hisses in a low grinding voice before it points an abnormally long finger at her, "None of your kind will. This is our time now and you all will die."

In a flash, it turns back into a mist and lunges at her like a raven-coloured fireball. Before it can get her at the last second, she flows through the open cabin door, gliding through the hole that leads to the surface of the ship. She manages to leave the sunken vessel for good but the shadow keeps catching up to her wherever she goes. No matter how many dives, flips, or swerves she does this thing keeps popping up in front of her.

As she continues to dodge the shadow, it mocks her, "You can swim but you can't hide!"

That is when she sees what could be her salvation: an old underwater church that she is certain no one has ever seen before. It is a big structure that still gleams white even with all the undersea growth on it. An ethereal light is shining down on it and Viola has a good gut instinct of what she must do. If she can not lose this demon, then she might as well defeat it herself.

The door to the church is open and as soon as she swims through it, she slams it shut before the creature can come through. As the demon bangs hard on the doors, Viola sees the light coming through the hole in the ceiling. It is so magical and beautiful that she feels safe despite the hell she is facing now. Perhaps this is the miracle that she needs. God knows she can't tell what this light is nor if it will help, but somehow, she has faith in it.

As the demon barges through the door, Viola hovers right where she is in the middle of the aisle. This demon suddenly makes itself a lot larger and stares down at her.

"Is that supposed to scare me?" She yells at the creature, "I am not afraid of you. You are nothing but a weak vile spook."

"How sweet." It talks down to her, "I do love it when the victim is spirited. You were terrific fun, but this little race of yours is over. Give me your soul!"

With that, the demon's face turns into a vile predatory expression with the razor teeth the size of an infant's arm and its eyes glowing red as it lusts for blood. Swiftly, Viola swims as fast as she can pass the light as this thing flies closely behind her.

As it passes through the light, it begins to scream as if it is in unbearable pain. Viola crashes herself into the wall as the demon roars out at her. With its contorted face pulling out of the light and close to her. It snaps its long teeth inches away from her face. In desperation, she turns her face away to keep it from getting at her.

As it let out a terrible scream, she shouts back at it, "GO TO HELL!!!"

Then suddenly, the shadow closes in on itself and completely disappears. Feeling herself relax, one muscle at a time, Viola takes a couple of minutes to rest and take in all that has happened. Soon, she decides that she must see her friends on the surface immediately and that the proper authorities can wait.

*****

At Elfina's house, Jacqueline and Meira sit on her kitchen chairs while Viola sits down on the ottoman in the living room. Elfina brings in hot hibiscus tea and lemon cakes for everyone. They have finished listening to Viola's account of what had happened to her under the sea. Jacqueline looks to Meira with a combination of wonder and fear in her eyes, while Meira shakes her head at this horrid situation, and Elfina just

140

stares at her friend with tears fighting to the surface of her eyes. The whole room is fearful for her safety.

The way that thing had chased Viola all over the sea and to the point of near exhaustion was more than anyone should handle. Elfina looks down at the tray of treats, feeling guilty about everything. She feels responsible for Viola's situation as it is the same if not similar to her own. Although it is unreasonable, she feels like she has put her friend in danger.

"Elfina?" Viola asks, blinking her slanted eyes at her friend with her own look of concern. She can feel the waves of depression off of her like the tides of the beach. "What's wrong?"

Looking shamefully back up at her friend, Elfina confesses, "This is my fault."

"What? How so, Sweetie?" Meira stands up quickly to walk over to put a tender hand on Elifna's shoulder.

"If this hadn't happened to me it wouldn't have happened to you." Elfina says to Viola, who crawls off of the ottoman to walk across to stand in front of her.

"Oh, Honey," Jacqueline speaks as she walks over to the other side of the nymph and puts a comforting cold hand on her other shoulder. "You didn't do this."

"Yeah Elfina." Viola takes the tray out of Elfina's hands and holds it. "This wasn't your fault. You didn't send these shadows after everyone."

"It was the necromancer's fault and no one else, okay?" Meira says in a rare show of kindness. Elfina nods and considers what all her friends are saying to her.

Elfina asks her friend again, "So how did you get out of that situation Viola?"

"Well, I saw this church…"

As Viola goes and puts the tray on the coffee table, she continues her story. Viola went on about swimming to the church and trying desperately to avoid the demon that was pursuing her. The women move all back to their seats. As they are sitting around her, they become intrigued when she mentions the light that came through the ceiling. Each one sits and sips their tea, paying close attention while focusing solely on Viola. For some reason, the light not only hurt the shadow beasts but it seemed to evaporate them entirely.

Elfina contemplates as she sips her tea and remembers something.

"At the very heart of the forest," Elfina mutters and has the woman look towards her.

"What do you mean, Elfina?" Meira inquires as she picks up a fork of her cake and bites into it.

"There is a light just like that here in the forest." She explains and stands up from her chair vigorously but still holds her tea with both hands without spilling a drop.

"In the heart of the forest." Elfina paces as she thinks out loud. "When I was still a small child, I saw this light. I was sad and thought there was no one to take care of me." Elfina pauses as she raises her hand for effect before continuing with her story. "I mean you guys know my parents. As gods they never took care of me, let alone approved of me. So, I wandered around feeling sorry for myself, and I found that light. It was shining down right in a clearing that is about five kilometres away from where my house sits now. I stepped into it and suddenly I felt like I knew what I had to do. It was like feeling a miracle for the first time."

"That must be why it worked for Viola." Jacqueline declares, "Besides don't they say in the bible, "Let there be light?""

"Must be the same thing" Viola pronounces with Meira nodding at her.

"Then there is only one thing I can do." Elfina sighs and gazes over to each of her friends. "I am going to lure this bastard into that light into the woods."

Her three friends look at her with wide eyes and open mouths. This is a revelation that they do not want to hear. The thought of their friend facing this thing alone should not be in the cards. Yet here she is stating just that.

Elfina looks at her friends' stunned faces and breaks the silence. "Guys you do know that this is the only way to get this creature out of my life."

Viola speaks up a little shyly. "We know that but Elfina…"

"Viola, you managed to get rid of your pursuer in your element of the sea." Elfina interrupts. "I am more than certain that I can get rid of them in mine which is the forest."

Although their faces completely change from surprise to something like understanding, each of the women feels their hearts sink into their bellies a little deeper.

"Still honey. Viola, although a wonderful swimmer." Jacqueline pauses as she waves a hand in the mermaid's direction. "Was lucky to get out of that alive. What will happen to you if we let you do this?"

"I don't know but I can't keep hiding from this. Something has to be done and clearly, this is what I have to do."

Meira who is uncommonly tacit finally speaks up. "You are right Elfina." As soon as she says this the whole room looks to her in utter astonishment. To placate everyone's stares at her she puts her palms up and out. "I know this is an ugly shock to me too but Elfina is not wrong. This shady prick is going to stalk her until it is destroyed."

After hearing this statement, Elfina's friends realize that it really is the only way to get rid of this demon. That does not mean that they like it. Elfina can see that they didn't due to the fact that they are all looking around at every other spot in the room other than directly at her. They are too afraid that she has to do this alone.

"Ladies, we all need to be prepared for what's coming." Elfina calmly tries to put her friend's mind at ease. "I suggest you guys get the men ready and get as prepped as possible. I'll meet you guys back here when I finish with that damned spook."

After they all leave the house, they walk to the pathway that leads to the different areas of the forest that they need to go. A wind blows from the south that feels cold, evil, and patient. All the women stand still in fear as they hear what seems to be a grizzly voice calling out Elfina's name.

"You don't have to do this Elfina." Meira puts a concerned hand on her shoulder, "I'm sure when we face that freak show at the mansion. It'll go away."

"Maybe but there is no guarantee of that and it would be better if we didn't have anymore interference." Elfina replies as she looks from the pathway to her friends, "Besides this thing has given us all enough grief and I am going to make sure that it is gone for good."

Meira nods while Jacqueline and Viola look at her with apprehensive expressions. Elfina grabs hold of Viola's and Meira's hands while the two of them hold onto Jacqueline's. With a deep inhale Elfina calmly looks into each of their anxious eyes.

"I'll see all of you soon at my store. I promise I won't be long."

"Be careful Elfina, and good luck." Jacqueline wishes as the rest of the friends nod in agreement.

With unhappy faces they all turn in the directions of their separate homes. Elfina begins to walk along the center path of the forest. For the first time in all of their lives and all of them not believing in doing such things, they pray that their best friend will be safe when they come back.

Elfina keeps on walking through the forest. With each step she struggles to ignore all the dark and fearful thoughts invading her mind by looking up at the rainbow of trees that normally make her so happy. Now they could be the last thing she ever sees. After she takes some deep breathes to calm her mind down, she wills this evil presence to come to her.

Suddenly in no direction that she can identify, comes a deep and dreadful growl. Elfina blinked her eyes for the longest five seconds of her life. She presses on and searches around for any kind of sign of the demon. She sees nothing but her gut tells her that this is only an illusion.

A rustle from the treetops behind her proves this as she spins around to look at the leaves in the tree ten feet away on the left move. It is as if there is a fierce creature skulking in it, waiting for the right moment to strike at some unassuming animal. It sends tremors up her back, but she continues to walk on as the treetops behind her continue to make the same noise. As soon as the tree beside her rustles she begins to pick up her pace. The plant still moves but she ramps up her speed and runs further into the forest. The shadow bursts out of the leaves to float from tree to tree to follow her.

Elfina seeing this thing close in on her did not dare stop as she sensed it coming closer and closer. In minutes it drops down to the ground gaining up on her like a flowing whisp of tobacco smoke. Even after she jumps over a log, and leaps over to a large rock, the shadow is still one step behind her. It is when she dodges its dive from the small hill, that Elfina realizes that she can not keep this up. After leaping off a rock it suddenly appears right in front of her. When it tries to grab her, Elfina curls herself into a ball and flips over the demon until she is behind it. It nearly grabs her with its long tentacle-like arm but with all her concentration, she freezes and turns into a bunch of bright-coloured wildflowers.

Once again, she has escaped and the shadow feels its rage bubbling inside of it. The demon snarls once more out of anger and lashes out at everything that is surrounding it. As if trying to destroy everything in its path the monster flails its tentacles at the trees and rocks. It does nothing to these objects. Only passes through them like a curl of nothingness. That is when it realizes that everything it is doing is useless.

The demon is losing its power and there is only one reason for that. It is no longer feared by its intended victim. As it still goes through its outburst, Elfina appears behind a tree, listening to its barking and screaming. Thanks to her nymph powers, she is able to travel herself like the roots of a plant through the soil and end up a short distance away. Albeit she is covered head to toe with soot and sweat.

When she rolls her eyes to look in front of her, Elfina sees the clearing that has the light through the forest treetops. Elfina sprints like there is no tomorrow towards that clearing. If she is going to get rid of this thing, she has to do it now. At least she can, thanks to this perfect shortcut.

The demon sees her run and flies after her at a furious speed. Swift enough to pick up her own stride, Elfina dashes into the clearing and glances up at the light that is just a few more steps before her. The twigs in the forest snap with the demon close behind her. Elfina detects the demon coming towards her.

She tries not to smile as she whispers in her mind, "That's right. Come to me, you spineless creep. Come to me."

As it hurries towards her with its sharp teeth showing and eyes glowing an angry red, Elfina jumps into the light when it is just a few inches away from her. A thud sounds as she hits the soft grass, lying flat on her back. She watches it scream in its horrible suffering, trying in vain to escape the painful prison that she had lured it to, but to no avail. The nymph continues to view it and thrash around until it finally disappears into nothingness and without a trace. She lifts herself slowly off the ground, looks around and then up to the light.

"How do you like that you bastard?" She speaks out loud as she brushes the dirt off her dress.

A deep breath escapes from her lips as Elfina leaves the clearing to go back to her house. The real battle is still ahead, and she knows that she has her work cut out for her. Fortunately, she is going in prepared.

Chapter Twelve

When Elfina returns home, she finds Javas and Viktor sitting on her front stoop waiting for her to return. The fey woman looks down at her dress and sees that she looks like she has just escaped from a battle even though that is exactly what she just did. Elfina brushes off whatever dirt that is left on her dress. Looking down at her sweaty hands and up at her arms which are equally dirty and scratched up, she realizes that she probably looks affright.

Never-the-less, she brushes her hand on her face and walks towards the two wizards with her head held high. They look at the disheveled nymph up and down in alarm. Viktor runs towards her as Javas follows closely behind, hobbling on his cane as fast as he can.

"Elfina!" Viktor calls as he puts his arms out towards her. "What on earth happened to you?"

"Oh, nothing just vanquished the demon that has been stalking me." She smiles at him and answers with an air of cheerful pride.

Viktor shakes his head at her and looks down before he speaks. "We came here because we are going with you to stop Enzor."

"What?" Elfina's breezy attitude changes to dread with her mouth open and voice low. "No you can't! You will be hurt."

"Maybe my dear," Javas says to her. "But this has to do with the brotherhood of wizards that both Viktor and I are a part of."

"Which is what exactly?" Elfina asks in an agitated voice raising her arms as if it is armor for an argument. "You two are not in any kind of club!"

"No not a club." Viktor replies keeping his voice even, "but wizards even independent ones like Javas and I have a responsibility. One of them is that if there are wizards using evil magic nearby then the other wizards must put a stop to it immediately."

"I can't let you do that." Elfina sadly drops her arms to her sides. "I can't lose you both either."

"My dear." Javas shuffles over to her and puts a comforting arm around her shoulders, leading her up her stoop and into her home. "Have a little faith. You know that this is bigger than all of us and like you, we have to do the right thing."

Elfina understands perfectly what he is saying but does not like it one bit. Her sad eyes say this more than her voice ever could. "Now why don't you go clean yourself up before you run into the lion's den? You maybe going into the big battle of the war, but you do not have to smell like it."

Elfina sticks her tongue out at the two of them and goes inside to follow this wise sage's advice. She is going to do that anyway but if there is anything that she hates as much as putting the people she loves in danger, it is being told what to do.

*****

At Elfina's store all her friends including the two elderly wizards are hunting for some much-needed items from her stock. Beside her tea shelves, Elfina grabs a jar of healing honey for wounds. She spins the jar with the golden liquid inside of it and studies it. Just a small dollop on the tongue and a person's wound will heal within 10-20 seconds. This depends on the size of the wounds.

After she puts it in her small knapsack, Elfina walks behind her counter to where her potion station is. She takes out a sprig of peppermint, a scoop of aloe gel, and a generous spoon of chili powder to put it into a tiny glass vial. She mixes the concoction by shaking her wrist and watches it change into a burgundy colour.

"Perfect," She thinks silently with a smile spreading on her face. This potion is the flawless counterbalance for poison. She puts this into her bag and quickly grabs some frankincense essential oil for protection against the dead.

Above all else, Elfina snaps her fingers as she remembers what else they need. Some angel grails will fully revive someone even if they die. Elfina had never been so grateful that she had fully stocked up on these defensive items. She grabs the small silvery cups with golden handles on each side and slides them carefully into her bag.

Now all they needed was the spiritual protection items that she had made a special point of ordering the other day.

"Okay Ozzie and I need those Ullr pendants, Elfina." With a nod, Elfina reaches up from her stepladder to her top shelf to grab a small wooden box. And just as Meira had asked for, she passed them the two small coins with the god of the hunt and journeys imprinted on them that lay impressively inside the box.

"Next!" Elfina yells out with a sassy look on her face as she steps down from the stool to deal with both Jacqueline and Stephan.

"Crosses for the both of us, please." Stephan orders playfully pointing his finger to the ceiling. She bends down at her jewelry countertop and passes the chained silver crosses to them. Elfina can't help snickering at the fact some people still think that crosses, silver or the combination of the two burn or keep both vampires and werewolves away. It never did but it is always fun when they go to these Earth Realm movies together. To watch the humans, think that this is of any use for defense against them.

For Viola she gets out the good luck and protection pendant of a jade green dragon. Seeing that she is of Asian heritage and still a believer (whether she admits it or not) the pendant is obvious.

As for Elfina, she pulls out a silver tree pendant that is of course perfect for a nymph. Since any members of the fey clan believe that anything in nature is a nurturer, provider, and guardian. With all their charms passed out, Elfina puts a crystal ball, a jar of will-o-the-wisps to light the way in a terribly dark place and a couple of vials of holy water to cause some serious damage to the demonic. Just in case this situation is heavier than they initially anticipated. Two is always better than one.

"Okay so we got the defensive items." Jacqueline announces impatiently, "How about some weapons?"

Looking over at the elves, Ozzie pipes up, "I thought you would never ask. Follow us."

*****

At the armory and weaponry shop, Ozzie passes around the weapons while Meira brings out some special armor that she had mentioned that she is working on. Elfina gets a couple of daggers with bright green ivy decorating the handles, Jacqueline has a long rapier with a gold handle, Stephan does not need anything, but Viola has a silver spear to strike hard and fast.

"Don't you just think you can just take over the world with weapons like these?" Elfina asks playfully at Jacqueline.

"Of course." She replies with a smirk of her own and the sarcasm to match as she swings her rapier side to side. "With weaponry like this we would be unstoppable but let's face it. In this case, we are the good guys."

Meira brings over the undergarment armor that she had specifically designed for wearing under clothing. Both the women and men put the armor on carefully. The metal molds against their bodies like it is a second skin. It may look like tin but it feels like silk.

"What is this, Meira?" Viola inquires, "It's wonderful."

"It's called Vertrene metal." Meira replies, "It's very light but it is stronger than any other basic metal. Secret to all the elves."

"Nice!" Stephan says as he is able to move easily in it. "It will stay on when I transform right?"

"It should." Ozzie answers as he gets the bow and arrows ready for Meira and twin swords as his weapons of choice, "It's not fragile by any means. A giant could punch you and you wouldn't feel it."

As the men continue to talk about the armor, Elfina looks outside the window and watches the sunset. She has faith that it won't be the last one she sees. However, that doesn't stop the nagging fear that is clenching her stomach at the moment. Javas and Viktor are waiting outside for them as they are already prepared for what is coming up. Taking a couple of deep relaxing breaths, Elfina walks back over to her friends. The men are still jumping around, pretending to fight each other, and just being silly as her friends watch them shaking their heads with laughter roaring from their lips.

Jacqueline notices that Elfina is unusually tense, so she puts her arms around her shoulders. "Problem Sweetheart?"

"No, it's just." She pauses to sigh and gather her thoughts, "I hate to think that this is the last time we all will be here enjoying these moments."

"We won't Babe." Meira assures her, "Now it's usually you who always says that there is always a happy ending to those who believe."

"I know but it was never this and it's usually something like the next business venture or a relationship thing." Elfina explains, "Not a battle between life and death or good and evil."

"Every bad thing that happens happens honey." Viola advises, "It's how you face it and move on from it that matters. You know that."

"I can't lose you guys though. I just can't." Elfina says simply as she looks down and tries her damnedest not to cry.

"Babe you won't. We will keep bothering you until the day you get sawed off somewhere." Meira tells her. "Have faith."

Elfina shakes her head and all her fears are finally silent. No more worries are going to plague her tonight. With determination, Elfina and the others wait for their carriage to arrive. They had called for it half an hour ago so it should be there any minute. And when it does, Enzor is going to get a taste of his own medicine.

*****

The house looks even more dead since the first time Elfina had seen it. It is darker and the walls are peeling large chunks of wood and decaying mold sits there like a grim evil. The dark grey house may have been dead looking but it somehow seems aware that they are there. A black curtain of translucent fog suddenly envelopes as if to ward them off. This is the house's aura, and it is so powerful that now it is showing itself off. Nevertheless, the eight of them walk towards the dismal hovel and into the front door that is rotting off its hinges.

The inside is worse than the outside. It is the very example of the house of Hades. Cobwebs are everywhere almost as if they are blocking the path. Water spots showed through the walls like black rotting eyeballs and just like the outside walls, they were decaying and peeling. The smell of death is everywhere and coming from more than one place. Walking into the hallway, they brush away the cobwebs and press forward. A rat runs across from one side of the hall to the other side. Viola gasps as soon as she sees it but covers her mouth to keep a scream from ringing out.

"Someone needs to clean up here," Jacqueline utters in disgust.

"It sure, as hell is not going to be me." Elfina answers and they continue down the entrance hall.

On the left of the hall, through an archway, they see what looks like what used to be a salon. It had old furniture turned over, a shattered coffee table, and what would have been a comfy fireplace is now cracked in two. As they walk on, Elfina looks at the room on the right. This clearly used to be the dining room with the long, solid wooden table and chairs. In the center of the table is a candelabra that is rusted over and filled with cobwebs. Elfina feels sad at seeing a house so neglected like this.

After what seems like it is too long of a time when it was only a few minutes, they finally reach some stairs. One stair is missing. The second, fifth, and sixth steps had holes in them. This is not going to be easy at all.

"Be careful everyone." Elfina cautions and starts to carefully climb the stairs. At this point she finds herself appreciative that she did not wear any high heels. She imagines the rest of her friends are thankful for that too. Not one of them would want to go through these nasty boards.

At the top of the stairs, they stop and look around at the second floor. It is no better than the first floor either. It is ceiling to floor, covered in dirt and dust with cobwebs raining down against the walls. However, that is not what first captures their attention.

There is a long line of doors on both sides of this hallway. The sensation of dread looms over all of them as if there is something waiting in these dark rooms. Whatever it is that is lurking in the shadows is waiting to jump out at them and rip them to pieces. Elfina pulls out the bottle of Will on the Wisps and shakes it as hard as she can for the lights to show the way with an amazing illumination.

Javas grabs her shoulder before she can lead the team down the corridor. He gives his warning, looking around at everyone else. "Stay close, everyone. They can't harm you if you stay in the light."

All of them begin to walk down the hall close behind each other. After walking past the first door, they all slam shut. Startling the whole group, they stop and watch as each door opens and slams shut by invisible hands. Over and over these doors bang with a cold hard vengeance. As they slowly walk forward the doors suddenly stop wide open and there in place of the unseen angry hands are the shadow demons. The black masses stand and watch all eight of them behind each door.

"Be careful, everyone." Viktor speaks up and puts both hands on Javas as he is starting to slump down on his walking stick. He closes his eyes and the way he keeps muttering quietly under his breath tells the group that he is speaking an incantation to protect everyone in the room against the dark forces. By the sight of him it is clearly exhausting him. Viktor continues his instruction while trying to assist Javas. "Now remember, don't acknowledge them or pay any mind to them. They will not bother us if we ignore them."

The wise rogue's advice is taken seriously as each member of the party moves forward until they come to the end of the hall facing the closed door. A sinister growl emerges before Elfina could reach for the doorknob. What looks like crawling flesh of different sorts, from Caucasian to dark skin, comes out of the cracks of the floor. The skins start to form a face. A big, round, horrific decomposing face with the odd skin patches squelching together, covering itself with puss. When the entity takes its form, it opens its eyes only to see pits of darkness within it.

"I am not one." It grumbles in a grizzly, gritty voice. "For I am many."

"Legion." Javas says in a near whisper. Legion grins menacingly, showing its blackened putrefied teeth before screaming a great wind at them that is meant to push all of them out of the house. One by one the group grabs onto a doorway, a knob or anything that would keep them from being blown away. Javas begins muttering a new spell to silence the beast's scream. With that, Legion no longer grins at them but looks over at the wizards with seething hatred.

"We will take care of it!" Viktor yells over to the rest of the party as he helps Javas to his feet. "Our magic will destroy it."

"But Viktor," Stephan shouts over to them.

"Don't argue, just go!" He screams back.

Knowing that there is nothing else that they can do, the six other mystics leave Javas and Viktor behind to kill the ferocious monster. They climb up the stairs to end the terror that swept itself into their lives. After all, this war is far from over. At the top of the stairs, the blood of the party freezes as they witness what is hiding in the darkness finally revealing itself to them.

Chapter Thirteen

The room is big and bleak. The stained-glass window in the shape of a dark star that is bleeding many colours is the first thing they see. The window reaches all the way from the ceiling to the ground, where a murky figure hovers over a table with wheels. The closer everyone looks, they see a man who is short, balding with black dyed hair, and standing over a corpse lying on a gurney. Slowly, he takes six-inch long thin needles and pokes them into the deceased's eyeballs. The man begins to speak in a low droning voice.

"ego dico nam longus mortuus phasma phasmatis de malum…"

Latin is not any of the group's strong knowledge, but it doesn't take a genius to guess what he is trying to do. The seven stretchers with the dead bodies covered in scars and pins say everything. He is trying to call on the dead to do his bidding which in turn opens a portal to the World of Darkness. The man stops what he is saying and looks up at the six of them. His eyes are dark and crazy just like the grin on his equally dyed black beard that curls under his pointed chin.

He stands up, raising his arms as if to brag about what he is doing when he speaks up to them, "Do you like my work?"

The group looks around at this evil lunatic's hole which is filled with bodies that have strange symbols on them and the bowls of dried blood that lay beside them. Now they study him and see that his clothes are just as rotted as the bodies in the room. He laughs out loud holding up the scalpel.

"I welcome you all and you will become a part of history." He articulates looking around at his pursuer's shaken faces, "A new kind of history."

Due to the grim and disgusting nature of this situation. No one knows what to think, but Elfina speaks up. "Why do this? What are you trying to accomplish?"

"Well, how do we always start a story again?" Enzor begins with a sickeningly smug smile and taps the scalpel to his demented lips, "Ah yes. Once upon a time, I was one of the top researchers at the Atlantis Institute and one of the best professors there. The people loved learning about the world's most dangerous beasts from this world, the Earth Realm, and the Dark Realm. But it was not enough. I needed to show the beasts from the Dark Realm to everyone. These beasts could be destroyed once and for all but of course the deans of the university were so concerned with the risks."

"So, you bring them out and have them attack people?" Jacqueline yells out at him pointing a long nailed red finger at him. In her ironic voice she continues. "Good idea. You have only killed so many innocents."

Jacqueline lowers her hand to step in and points her rapier towards him.

"Am I finished talking little girl?" Enzor annoyedly points his long finger back at her. He declares, "Lets close those gorgeous fangs of yours and keep your mouth shut!"

Out of his finger comes a dark snake-like cloud, that wraps itself like a stitching needle through Jacqueline's mouth at the speed of a sewing machine. With what is left over of his magic, Enzor has Jacqueline's rapier float up in mid-air. First it went towards him and then it pointed in the direction of the six. It soars in their direction but with a little luck, they dodge the weapon. Promptly it pierces the top of the doorframe that they have entered from.

With her red lips completely sewn over, she puts her fingers over her mouth and the group's concerned eyes fall on her. Elfina kneels down as Jacqueline does and tries looking at her mouth while her husband puts his arms around her. Meira and Viola are still standing but circle in front of her to see if she is alright. Ozzie just stares at the necromancer.

"Now as I was saying," He continues as they all turn to face him with pure distinct anger as he speaks. "Now they all caught me bringing out one beast, calling it malevolent practice and they fucking threw me out. Now I was not only a laughing stock but I lost everything! My wife, my home, everything! So now I am going to prove them wrong and they will beg me to come back. And when they do, I will set these shadows after them for their own treachery."

He giggles in sickening delight after he shares his story with them. It only made them pity this pathetic wanna-be hero. So sick of hearing the ramblings of a nutcase, the women stand up and walk towards him. He stops them by raising his palm out towards them and lets out another quick chant that they don't understand. A sudden rustling noise sounds behind them, and the many bodies on the floor come to life right before their eyes. The dead bodies all howl out towards them and begin to limp and lurch towards them.

"Now, I am sure since you are my guests, you will want a little company." He verbalizes evenly as he waves the zombies forward.

"Get him. We'll take care of the corpses." Ozzie shouts out to Meira as Stephan jumps behind the group to let out a howl of his own.

They watch as he transforms himself into a wolf-creature with his big long claws, furious furry face, and gigantic muscles growing out that are completely covered with hair. Werewolf Stephan makes the first move, pouncing on the one zombie that is approaching the group. When he finishes ripping the zombie apart, he tears into the others that start coming close to him. Ozzie jumps into the fray with his twin swords and begins to slash at every undead pursuer that moves in on him with incredible swiftness. The women turn to the necromancer and walk towards him with some heavy-duty anger aimed towards him.

He has an angry streak of his own as he moves surgical instruments with his mind like he did with Jacqueline's rapier, from the table towards them. The women duck down just in time before anything could hit them.

Enzor raises his hands and with a low droning voice says, "Invoco tenebras." He looks towards the woman with a lurid, crooked grin. "May the dark wind pull you all into its embrace."

At the top of the ceiling comes a small but strong indoor tornado before the window. The funnel brings up some of the corpses but Meira manages to jump behind the wicked wizard and grabs him before he finishes the invocation. The storm disappears but the zombies still regenerate and come after the two men trying to fight them off.

Viola is so tired of it all and filled with so much debilitation of all the evil surrounding her and interfering in her friends' lives. With tears and sweat running down her face, she screams with all her might. "In the name of god, stop!!"

And that is exactly what happens. Everything suddenly stops as if time freezes. The zombies turn and face an angry-eyed, tear-stained Viola. The men manage to stop ripping the zombies apart. When Stephan turns back into his human self, they both look at her with stunned eyes. With everyone staring at her, Viola looks around the room and shrugs her shoulders, feeling somewhat confused.

*****

One floor down, the fatigued wizards have nearly finished off the equally exhausted monster. Javas leaned heavily on his staff with his eyes closing slightly and being out of breath. Viktor is having a hard time standing with his back hunched over and bracing himself on his knees looks glaringly at his opponent before him. Legion's face is already cut up and showing off the signs of its weariness. Javas puts his free hand on Viktor's shoulder to stop him from casting another spell on it when he realizes that it isn't moving anymore.

Legion turns its gaze upwards. Its face begins to melt with a black mass coming out of its eyes and ears before it completely disappears. The two of them stop to analyze why this has happened. However, they can find nothing here to suggest why that would suddenly occur like this. So, there is only one thing to do. Viktor and Javas head upstairs as fast as they can. They look around and see that the zombies are standing still like statues staring straight at Viola.

"What did you do?" Viktor asks with a raised eyebrow at Viola.

"I don't know I just screamed at them to stop and they did." Viola explains as she looks around the room, wide-eyed and shaking like a trapped rabbit. "And now they are just staring at me and it's freaking me out."

Elfina runs over to the dark wizard with her dagger in hand and yells. "Let them go! These innocent souls that you brought back are tormented enough. LET THEM GO!!!"

Waving the dagger threateningly in front of his face, he looks her straight in the eye and shouts back, "They are mine, forever! I will get my revenge no matter what I have to do to get it. You jumped up bastards will never learn."

Elfina knows what he means when he says that. To kill this man is not the answer nor is it her style. She remembers Javas' teachings about necromancers: that killing him especially in a malevolent way would only make things that much worse by making him more powerful. His power comes from death, so if death is put upon him, he gains more of it. But she did have something that will make him suffer. She takes out the vial of holy water from her pack and gestures it in front of his face.

"What is that?" He growls at her.

"Take a guess genius." She snaps sharply back at him.

"You keep that away." He fearfully panics as fear writes itself on his face.

"No."

Elfina immediately sprinkles the heavenly liquid all over his body. He screams to the top of his lungs like he is getting sprayed with acid. His skin turns red and blisters on his already wretched face. This should release the zombies from their evil magic. When she takes the second vial of holy water out, he snivels a small quiet incantation. She looks over to the zombies and they fall to the ground like they were never walking around to begin with.

When Viktor runs over to Viola, Javas hobbles over to Elfina. "How did you know the holy water would work?"

Elfina turns and explains to him, "Well I think it was when Viola said the word *god* that caused all the zombies to stop. So, figuring this man was never baptized by any means, I took the holy water and silently baptized him."

Viktor raises an eyebrow at her and announces smugly, "Sounds simple don't you think?"

"That's why we can get the Knights and Valkyries here to get rid of the rest of this mess." Viola chimes in.

Elfina gets up as Jaqueline rushes over and starts scratching at the dark wizard due to her predicament. It is not just the zombies that need to be released.

With Stephan and Ozzie stepping in to stop her, the two men pull her off the severely injured wizard. Jacqueline starts jumping up and down, trying to scream, and pointing at her stitched mouth. She looks like a sleek sewn cat with her angry claws out. With her husband holding onto her, she keeps furiously trying to tell them something.

"Here dear," Viktor says walking over to her. "Let me help you."

With Viktor muttering the counter spell for Jacqueline, everything is safe now. Elfina meditates her message to the telepathic operators for the right powers-that-be to come as fast as they can.

*****

In a matter of minutes, the place is swarming with Knights, Valkyries, Bishops, and Exorcists from all regions of the realm to lift the bad vibes of this place and secure Enzor. What was once a bloody nightmare is now finally over. Thanks to all of these workers who are riding the last of the bad jujube in the house with Viktor and Javas assisting them.

As Stephan and Ozzie have already given their statements, they had left over half an hour ago. The four women who have dealt directly with Enzor for most of the night are standing together, giving the head Knight his floating parchment notepad and quill feverishly writing their account of the events. "We have everything we need. You ladies can go home now."

With that, they link their arms and all walk together towards the carriages that the red-headed Valkyrie is waving down for them.

"God when I get home, I am going to have a long hot bath with jasmine and eat a chocolate mousse the size of my head." Elfina breaks the silence with a smile.

"What no champagne Elfina?" Meira sarcastically suggests.

"Absolutely, that my dear goes without saying," Elfina answers as she runs a hand through her mussed-up hair. "What about you girls?"

"Go home and have some hot sex with my man." Meira answers as she looks over to Jacqueline.

"Same here." She agrees with her friend but presses some gentle fingers to her still-sore lips. "But I am so not doing anything with my mouth."

As soon as she said that all the women turned and looked at her in surprise. Elfina chortles. "Having your lips zipped gets you going, does it?"

Jacqueline blinks at her and shakes her head with an impish smile crossing her face.

"I plan on kissing both of my parents, eating the most delicious crab cakes in the sea, and explaining to my boss why I could not get down to business with him tonight."

All of them started to laugh at her while Elfina could not help but speak up. "God! Prim and proper on the outside but inside completely and utterly dirty."

"I'm not dirty." Viola stares daggers at Elfina, blushing. "It was a business meeting."

However, everyone has to agree with Elfina. Viola allows a chuckle to escape from her lips while they all still laugh and playfully push each other. When the carriage pulls over and picks up these disheveled and dirty women who gleefully climb up inside, as all of them enter the carriage, each one gets comfortable in the velvet pillowlike seats. A yawn escapes Viola's mouth while Elfina flutters her eyes closed. Without meaning to, she falls fast asleep. Meira presses her knuckles to her forehead and finds herself drifting off while Jacqueline looks over to her sleepy companions. She can't help but think that now she is happy that this whole mess is over and done with. Their lives are safe at last.

*****

Over the next few days, Enzor is awaiting his punishment in his dank, dribbling prison cell. He has been sitting day in and day out with the sun beating down on him like a spotlight through the small barred window above him. It makes him sick to his stomach feeling this warm stream of light. There is no one around this cold, clammy little cage and the boredom is almost unbearable.

Waiting for his death sentence is just as painful as thinking of the death itself. No one has told him what his punishment is going to be like. What he does know is that the psychic across from his cell doesn't know either. For some reason the grand diviners have found a way to completely block off precognitive abilities so no one would know what awaits them.

Grand diviners are the highest form of holy mages who have mastered the mystic arts that took centuries to achieve. Magic in all its forms lies in all things. It can only be unlocked by doing good deeds and belief in oneself with the mindfulness that life is unpredictable and vast.

This is a way of these special magicians. It is not an easy position to get in any realm. In fact the few that do achieve this are highly respected and famous masters of magic.

There is a knock on the metal bars of the jail. A tall and muscular beast man with blonde hair walks in and stoically calls to him, "Time to go."

The magical metal shackles appear on his hands and feet as the doors to his cell open wider. The furry man lifts his crinkled face in the air and sniffs. He senses that the room is ready and waiting for this criminal to face what is coming to him. The man takes Enzor's arm vigorously forcing the necromancer down the corridor until they reach the ancient and rusted over steel door at the end of it.

In the beast man's native tongue, he speaks incoherent growing words. "Bruff unga chii yago una."

The door turns its rusted wheel and removes the thick ragged locks. It opens to a round room that looks like a dome with high stone walls and arches. In the room stands three sorcerers dressed in black necked robes decorated with jewels of every color. Together they were quietly chanting an incantation. The three of them bow after they finish, turn, and face the two men who are at the door. The three of them are bald with black goatees and their eyes are different colors from one another.

The blue-eyed man slowly approaches the necromancer. "You have spoken to the holy men?"

"Yes." Enzor grumbles. The more he looks at these men the more the fury inside of him erupts, "How is what I did any different from what you men do?"

The golden-eyed man advances to Enzor and informs, "We don't summon evils from the demonic world, nor do we send them to hurt others."

The last sorcerer with green eyes walks towards him and tells him the rest. "The black mirror is ready. We must leave immediately."

The wizards bow to the beast man and he in turn nods in understanding before he pushes Enzor into the room. He turns around to leave the room with the wizards following close behind him and leaves Enzor to the mirror. The magical shackles on his extremities disappear into thin air. He wrings his wrists in relief after being freed from them.

In a few seconds he begins to examine the odd-looking mirror. It has an eerie beauty that any man, evil or not would want to possess it. Other than that, it is just like a plain ordinary-looking glass. He wonders why they would leave him alone with it as he studies the intricate detail of the frame. It resembles a cross between black slithering snakes and dark flames blazing up to the sky with black skulls on the bottom.

Suddenly a small blue flame appears in the center of the mirror. It is like a tiny blue sensual dancer trying to tempt him to come closer. Enzor squints his eyes at it and finds that this flame is steadily growing into something bigger. It only takes a few seconds before the flame starts to spin into a black hole with actual flames appearing randomly in it. Startled, Enzor backs away slowly from the mirror as he watches this black hole fill up the entire reflective surface. His skin tingles until he feels it crawl. Enzor runs to the door to bang on it.

"Let me out! Let me out!" He begs with tears streaming down his red wrinkled face until he starts to demand. "I don't want to be in here! Don't you know who I am?"

The four of them stand at the other side of the door, saying nothing. The beast-man gazes at his jagged claws. He realizes that he has to make an appointment with the manicurist to get them cleaned up. The three men on the other hand have their eyes closed and silently hum as if they are out of their bodies. Either way no one is opening that door.

Enzor gives up on slamming his bruised and bloody fists on the door. A strange static noise comes out of the mirror, which causes the scared little man to look over his shoulder to watch helplessly as the mirror changes once again. The black hole with flame pits starts to come out from the mirror and shapes itself into a big clawed hand that reaches out for him. He lets out a scream of true terror as the hand closes in around his waist and pulls him inside. When he is completely gone, the mirror slowly morphs back into its normal self.

In the corridor the beast man asks the wizards, "So did they take care of that evil shit back at that manor?"

"Yes." The green-eyed man explains, "We took care of the bodies."

"We had to do a few incantations and some potions but we did manage to get rid of all the symbols on those poor carcasses." The golden-eyed sorcerer continues.

"Yes, and sent them back to their graves in the Earth Realm." The last wizard finishes. "They are good as new."

The beast-man nods at them. "Making dead bodies into new ones?" He shakes his head in a confused manner. "What about all the bad vibes and spirits?"

"The holy men took care of all that." The blue-eyed one announces. "From all religions just in case."

"And they got some handymen and tradesmen working on that house to fix everything up." Says the golden eyed wizard.

"Oh? To make it look nice again?" The beast man inquires and is answered with nods. "So, you guys wanna go out and get a couple of beers?"

The three black-cladded sorcerers look at each other as if to come to some kind of telepathic understanding. With that they nod at him.

"We believe that would be a wise choice in our situation." The golden-eyed wizard announces.

With a "wise" decision made, the four of them walk out of the corridor to leave the building.

*****

Enzor is pulled into the Dark Realm after the black hole drops him on the ground. He feels nothing but sand and sees nothing but pitch black surrounding him. He can not see where he is or where he has come from. But he decides that crawling around might get him somewhere or so he hopes. He does not get far when he puts his hand in a strange, warm liquid, which is an unusual change from the cold he feels under his other hand.

He brings his hand close to his face to inspect it. The feel of it between his thumb and forefinger feels viscous and sticky. He puts it to his nose and gives it a sniff. The metallic smell of it tells him all he needs to know. His hand is covered in blood. As he whimpers, he hears something large and vicious coming for him. The problem is he doesn't know where it is coming from.

Suddenly he is impaled with something big and sharp going through the middle of his back. With his eyes fearfully closed, he pops them open to find that he is still alive despite this large sharp object going through him.

Despite feeling a pain that he has never felt before, Enzor turns his neck around and looks agonizingly up. He sees a giant arachnid with crustation-like claws, steely shimmering blue eyes, and fangs more ferocious than any creature he had ever seen before. Immediately, he remembers what it is.

"Arach." He whispers in fear as the thing looks down at him with its eyes reflecting the man who is stuck on its leg.

When it lets out a big hiss, it moves forward again as the necromancer screams in anguish. "You fucking bastards! Damn, you Atlantis! Damn you Knights and Valkyries! Damn you four interfering women and your men! I will destroy you all yet!"

As he travels in this eternal pain, he does not realize that making threats and willing ill in the Dark Realm means absolutely nothing. Just more pain that comes to those who do bad things is one of the first karmic rules. The one thing that Enzor never learned and never will now is that he lives in a trap in a hell of his own making.

Epilogue

October 31 is a big night for the Nether Realm. What is Halloween in the Earth Realm is the celebration of the Centennial Festival here. And it has everyone happy because for this one night, all night, worlds are together and they celebrate life, both natural and supernatural.

Most businesses have closed to get ready for the evening as it will be pure excitement for everyone including the entertainment which gets different and more extravagant every single year. The food, the dancing, and what people are wearing are just some of the highlights of the evening.

Back at her store, Elfina dresses beautifully in a low-cut, peek-a-boo, oriental-style dress that looks like a multicolored galaxy as she is just finishing up with her ledgers. She can't wait for tonight. The anticipation in her has her nearly jumping out of her chair. For this reason, she had promised herself earlier that she would finish her work as early as possible. As she puts her accounting book at the top of the shelf, Meira comes in through the front door.

"So, are you coming or what?" Meira bounces excitingly up and down sharing in the enthusiasm of the festival.

"Yeah, I'm just getting ready to close shop." When Elfina turns around she sees a sight on Meira that would stop anyone in their tracks. "Oh my god! You are *wearing* a dress!"

Meira looks down her long white dress with silk and lace at the bust and some strappy high-heeled sandals on her feet. "Go figure huh?"

"What's the occasion?" Elfina asks slyly looking at her normally tomboyish elf friend.

"Oh, lets see," Meira answers in an acerbic girly fashion. "Well, it's not the Centennial festival or the fact that I wanna go party nor is it

169

the fact that I am glad that this whole Enzor mess is over so everyone can enjoy themselves again."

"Sounds like a good excuse to me." Elfina says as she fluffs up her French twist with a single strand of hair coming out of the top.

"Of course not." Meira speaks as she pulls the nymph off the stool, "So come on let's go party!" After they both laugh, Elfina allows herself to be dragged off to the party.

Glad to be going to the party of the year. Elfina and Meira walk towards the destination where it's being held. It has always been where all beings of the Nether Realm consider the center of the world which by happy coincidence is just outside of Merkiva. For that reason, it would not take them long to get there and they really couldn't wait. By the way they are giggling and practically skipping to the location.

"So, what's the first thing you are going to do Meira?" Elfina asks hyped up on so much exhilaration.

"That's a no-brainer," Meira replies to her. "I'm going to grab a beer and meet Meg the Amazon who beat the shit out of that giant in the recent Colusa fight."

"Why did I ask?" Elfina sighs with a hint of sarcasm as she shakes her head and smiles.

"Why? What are you going to do?" Meira questions in a mocking tone. "Watch the fire eater make shapes out of fire? Oh! I got it! You're going to see who won the best decorated tree."

"Actually, I am hoping to get the dancing going but that won't happen until sundown so I think I'll take in the latest gossip."

"Ah! I can tell you that right now." Meira states and lets her annoyance show with the situation. "Those Knights and Valkyries are taking credit for our saving the world from Enzor and his shadow goons."

"It was for our own protection." Elfina corrects as she puts a calm hand on top of her friends. "I have to admit they were right when they said that people would constantly bang on our doors and even some other wackos will try and track us down."

"In other words, good business." Meira jokes at that. *It is so true,* Elfina thinks.

"So, when do you think Viola and Jacqueline will get there?" Meira asks her after she calms down from the combination of annoyance and amusement.

"They are already there. Viola said that she wanted to get there early and Jacqueline wanted to show off her latest artwork."

"Makes sense." Meira walks on arm and arm with her friend but finds herself having to ask. "You're not going to dance all night, are you?"

"Well maybe I'll get lucky." Elfina seductively winks at Meira.

"Oh?" Meira smiles playfully back at her friend, "Premonition?"

"No guarantee." With both women giggling they both pace to the festival with joy and confidence.

*****

A few hours into the festival, the four lady friends are standing in their circle chatting, drinking, and enjoying the sights around them. Jacqueline wears a black dress suit with lacy pantyhose and pointy high-heels while Viola dresses in a lovely vintage peach dress with a shell headdress on her head and white flats. Suddenly when the trumpets hit the top notes, the ladies smooth over their dresses.

The fire eater has just finished their show and now comes the real entertainment. Dragons of every species and color swoop down with their riders performing stunts to music.

It is so much more than majestic; it is pure magic. The dragons swoop, aerial all over the sky, and even did a series of loops. It looks almost like riding a roller coaster but this time magic lights trail with them and the dragons are decorated in jewels. As the dragons come together facing back-to-back with each other breathe their separate elements of fire, ice, and thunder outside the circle. These performers fill the sky with a rainbow of wonder.

Elfina spots Haroun and his red dragon Asheem in the sky. She points out to them showing her group, and they all watch. He and Asheem perform their tricks and maneuvers for all to see. They start with a dive and move in a zigzag pattern across the sky until they form together in a circle with the other dragons. It is as if they are totally in sync with each other. The dragon and his rider, ride the sky and light up everyone's enthusiasm with all the other dragons.

"He is the best one," Jacqueline announces suddenly.

"I agree." Viola sips on her white wine.

"Ditto." Meira toasts up to the sky with her beer mug.

Elfina just titters in response to them and looks back up at the sky.

"I guess his dragon isn't so horny after all," Jacqueline whispers to Elfina, "Right dear?"

"Not as defiant, that is for sure," Elfina snickers, "but Asheem seems happier too."

Nodding at that, Jacqueline puts an arm around her friend's shoulder as they continue to watch the dragons in the sky.

Before the next rousing show starts, the ladies stroll over to the liquor stand and buy their preferred beverages each. More blood for Jacqueline, white wine for Viola, a beer for Meira, and red wine for Elfina. As they finish their orders, Viktor, his wife and Javas come towards them and greet one another.

"Javas!" Elfina excitedly gives him a brief hug. "I didn't think you would come."

"Well, I would regret it if I didn't come up for air, especially for an event like this."

With his arm around Maddy, Viktor lifts his glass to the four women and asks, "So having fun yet ladies?"

"Yes," Meira replies quickly before the others do. "And you, Sir Viktor? Are you behaving?"

He looks down at his near silent but cranky-faced wife and smiles. "I'm trying not to but Maddy won't let me."

She waves her hand at him and she pipes up in her gruff voice, "Ah! You know no manners Fool!"

They couldn't agree more with Maddy as they all laughed. She doesn't speak to them often but when she does, she always knows how to make marital spats comical. As she treats them to a crooked smile of her own and a hard laugh, they all toast each other.

The loud sound of the bullhorn gets everyone's attention. The satyr emcee announces on the stage. "And now for our next magical show, a tale as old as antiquity itself, presented by the Fey Ballet Troupe "The Origin of the Fairies.""

Together the women watch the beautiful ballet unfold in front of them. A glittering background of flowers spreads across the night like a sparking curtain. The fairies that burst out from these florae sparkle even more than the 3-D backdrop that they are dancing around.

Both Stephan and Ozzie move a little closer to look under one of the dancers. The two of them pass each other some gold pieces and fist bump each other on some unknown agreement.

"What are your fellas doing down there, girls?" Viktor asks with a grin on his face as he watches them exchange money.

"Placing bets." Jacqueline says as she takes a sip of her drink and watches her husband plot with his friend, "They are hoping that one of the fairies will accidentally flash a little something, something."

"Well hell." Viktor says as he walks over to them. "I'll place a little wager on that."

Shaking her head, Maddy once again replies. "Men."

All the women and Javas laugh as they watch the three of them exchange the gold pieces in their pockets. Knowing that there is no chance of them seeing any kind of nudity during this show, they still hope that one day it will happen. Javas hobbles over to sit on a boulder, and the rest of them still stand to view the ballet. As the men cheer on for certain possibilities, Viola can only shake her head at them.

"What?" Elfina exclaims as she looks at the slightly irritated Viola.

"Oh, the three of them!" Viola tells her shaking her head. "Why must they always hope that one of these wonderful women has to take her top off?"

With a roll of her eyes, Elfina bursts out.

"Let them dream. Besides they will get to see naked women after this is all over right Jacqueline and Meira?"

"Of course." They both say in union and chuckle.

"But we won't make it easy." Jacqueline points out to the rest of her friends.

"Damn straight." Meira declares. "So, Viola where is your lucky guy?"

"He's around here somewhere." She looks down at her drink while a flush shows on her face. "I don't think it's going to work out though."

"Why?" Elfina asks.

"I just don't see any kind of future with him." Viola shrugs her shoulders.

"Oh, honey so you didn't even bring a date to this thing?" Jacqueline inquires.

"I said I didn't think we had a future together not that I am a fool." Viola smugly raises an eyebrow then looks remorsefully over to Elfina. "I'm sorry."

"Don't worry about it." Elfina waves her hand at her. "Besides there is someone here I am supposed to meet anyway."

"Yeah, a premonition about a man she is going to bring home." Meira winks at them.

"Oh, that's good. It has been a while since you have been with someone." Jacqueline toasts her with her wine glass of blood.

Elfina shakes her head at her friend. She considers herself an independent woman who doesn't need a man to make her happy, but she is a woman still who has some needs to meet. So, tonight is the night for that, and it is not unusual on this night for these sexual needs to be met. When those musical instruments are heard that means that the dancing and fireworks are about to begin.

"Come on ladies let's hit the floor!" Elfina salutes as the rest of her friends hop to.

The ground lights up and sparkles in a collage of colors while the flames begin to glow around the parklands and the music soars joyfully in the air. Everyone moves and shakes in high spirits into the night as they stomp to the drums, jump to the sound of the guitar, and live for the moment.

As soon as the first slow song starts Jacqueline and Meira dance with their lovers while Viola dances with her date. Elfina looks out at the bystanders and sees a familiar friendly face in the distance. It is Tommy, his wife, and their infant son sitting on a picnic blanket. With a smile, Elfina decides to give Tommy his promised dance.

Elfina goes through the crowd of dancers and up to Tommy. With a gentle curtsey she requests, "May I have this dance?"

A grin spreads on his face and gives her a nod. "I was wondering when you were going to ask."

With a tender pat on his shoulder, Tommy's wife looks lovingly at him. "You're lucky I'm not the jealous type."

He lets out a chuckle and pulls her close to give her a peck on the cheek. Elfina could not help but blush and look starry-eyed at the two of them. They are so cute. As the soft sound of the flute moves around them, Tommy and Elfina share a friendly dance with his hands on her waist and her arms resting on his shoulders.

Felling a sudden bump against them, Elfina finds herself face to face with a handsome angelic looking elf. "Oh, please excuse me."

Elfina checks him out coquettishly and smiles. "It's alright. It's nice to meet you."

"Sorry?" The mysterious suitor asks her.

"Oh! We didn't introduce ourselves, did we?" Elfina inquires before Tommy interrupts.

"Okay. I can take a hint." Tommy says, giving her a little smack on her bottom. "Have fun tonight dear."

The mystery man holds his hand out to Elfina and gives her a bow, showing his gentlemanly nature. Elfina gives him a curtsey and lightly places her hand in his. She finds herself being swept away into a lovely slow dance. A perfect way to start a little romance.

He smiles at her as they dance, but like anything else, the two of them begin a conversation.

"Aaron." He announces.

"Elfina." She responds.

With her arms resting on his shoulders and his hands gently on her waist, the two of them gaze at each other even though Elfina breaks the silence

"You look like you had the day off today."

"Oh? What makes you say that?"

"The beautiful Victorian suit that you are wearing." Elfina chuckles at him. "It looks extremely pristine."

Aaron returns the chuckle and informs her. "I stopped in my lodge just to drop off my reports. I work as a forest ranger."

"Oh?" Elfina lifts an eyebrow at him, showing an interest. "I love a man who works with nature."

With a few words they are sharing, Elfina's moss green eyes gaze wistfully into his lake-blue eyes. Before she can even think of it, she finds herself swept away in a petite passion. She considers herself one lucky girl. She has her three best friends, a great business, and now it looks like an exciting new man in her life.

There is no happily ever after here, at least not yet. Because this story isn't over. In fact, it is only the beginning.

Manufactured by Amazon.ca
Bolton, ON

40600947R10098